DANDRE WALKER

The Man Across Eight Mile

FLORENCE
WOODWARD
PUB

First published by Florence Woodward Publishing 2021

This novel is entirely a work of fiction. The names, characters and incidents portrayed in it are the work of the author's imagination. Any resemblance to actual persons, living or dead, events or localities is entirely coincidental.

Designations used by companies to distinguish their products are often claimed as trademarks. All brand names and product names used in this book and on its cover are trade names, service marks, trademarks and registered trademarks of their respective owners. The publishers and the book are not associated with any product or vendor mentioned in this book. None of the companies referenced within the book have endorsed the book.

First edition

ISBN: 978-1-73-310102-8

This book was professionally typeset on Reedsy.
Find out more at reedsy.com

This book is dedicated to all my grandparents. Cheryl Cornish, Leroy Cornish, Doris Walker, Sherrill Perry & Essie Tipton. It is especially dedicated to Grandma Cheryl, who often sits with me for hours and gives details about her youth. A collection of all of their stories and journeys in Detroit and in the South, shaped some of the characters, events and setting in this book and helped to make it authentic.

1

Chapter 1

The first time you hold a gun to someone's head will almost certainly never be your last. I won't say that it's easy to even come close to taking someone's life, that would make me a monster. But the right reasoning, made it a lot easier. There are two types of killers out there. Those that get a rush off the godlike power, and those that regret it and never fully accept what they've become. I've known both very well.

My first time, I was about twenty years old and ten thousand miles away from home. I had been in Vietnam for three days when we got a tip from one of the South Vietnamese soldiers that some of the villagers had been harboring and feeding some Vietcong. It was finally time for some action and we were sent in to flush them out.

We rolled up there all strong and mighty with the morning sun rising behind us. Our vehicles trampled anything in our path. Guns out, Jeeps rolling. From a mile off, the villagers must have seen us. They scattered like roaches and disappeared into the vegetation, hoping we would leave them be. I'm sure their hearts dropped when we pulled up to the main road in front of the village.

One of our South Vietnamese translators was named Chi. He hopped down from the jeep. He strolled towards the village with a calm confidence. Lieutenant told him what to yell out.

"Come on out. If you don't we'll burn this whole thing down." He sounded like some mythical animal as he screamed out.

The Lieutenant wasn't a patient man. He called out to Private Schultz, this white boy from Memphis. Tall. Strong. A look of fire in his eyes. That flame thrower belonged in his hands more than any other place in the world. If he didn't join the Marines, I'm sure he would've been welcomed into some looney bin. My heart thumped as he ran up, and aimed that fire stick.

At the last second, a short man came to the door. Around five-four, maybe. He wore nothing but a pair of pants. His fighting days were way behind him. His aged eyes stared at us. We must've been scarier than death itself, especially Schultz, who was itching to burn some shit up.

The old man limped out to us and began to talk to the Lieutenant through Chi. After a few seconds, the Lieutenant sent us in to inspect the homes and keep anything we found. Tiny dogs ran around the yards yapping at us. If you let them get really close, they'd nip at your boots. I guess they knew who the trouble was. A good hard kick was enough to get them to back off.

I walked with who would become a good buddy of mine, Private Jason Everett. His M16 shook just as hard as mine. We bent down and entered a hut. Nothing but women, children and a few elderly all huddled up in a corner. We ordered them out and that's when the crying began. I guess they knew the drill. Oh you'd have to be a cold son of a bitch to not have felt anything in that moment.

We led everyone in town to the center of the road and made them sit down in the heat. They squinted their eyes in the direct sunlight. Two guys called out to the Lieutenant. They found some rice that had been stored away. The Lieutenant looked like his heart had been broken.

He yelled out "Why'd you lie to me?" to the old man. That translator could've won an Oscar for his performance. He seemed even angrier than the Lieutenant. The old man was crying out that they hadn't seen any soldiers for months and how the rice was for his people. Always skeptical, the Lieutenant wasn't buying it. The tension was thicker than the suffocating humid air. It increased as the younger women held back their older counterparts from running to the old man's aid.

The Lieutenant looked over at Schultz. "Burn it down," he said, his voice cold. The old man dropped to his knees and tugged at the bottom of Chi's olive green shirt. I didn't need a translator to know what he was saying but what happened next shocked me. The Lieutenant called me over to him.

My heart pounded and I stood still until he yelled at me again. I ran over to him. My legs almost gave out under the heavy gear. He stared in my eyes as he gave the order for me to shoot the man.

I froze up. I thought we were supposed to only shoot soldiers. Why did he pick me to do this? This man had to be seventy. I couldn't believe it. I took the pistol from the Lieutenant. The old man's eyes pleaded not to. But at the same time, they were accepting. He was willing to die right then and there.

I looked back at the platoon. They were a mixed bag. Some had been there long enough that it didn't bother them. Others had been told to do similar things. It was an initiation process.

I turned back to the man. I had never felt so weak in my life. It was almost as if I had no control of my body.

I closed my eyes and squeezed the trigger. Lieutenant didn't say where to shoot him so I shot his thigh. I was softer then.

The Lieutenant reached down to the man's thigh and dabbed his fingers in the gushing blood. He held them up to the company and exalted.

"We got a live one boys, looks like he just popped his cherry."

They cheered and ran up and rubbed my back. I'd never forget the look on a little girl's brown face. A petrified look of horror, as if she had seen demons. Maybe she had.

That was the first gunshot I heard in Vietnam. Not a fire fight between soldiers, but an old man taking a bullet in his thigh.

Once you cross that threshold of pointing a gun at someone, it almost always happens again. There's no going back to what you were before. There were good reasons for pointing guns at people. And there were bad reasons. Sometimes the line between the two was blurred.

2

Chapter 2

I had been waking up with Stevie Wonder the past few weeks. Songs in the Key of Life had come out a few weeks before. It was so influential that my wife felt the need to buy a whole new God damn record player just to hear it on. Of course she put it right in our room. Every morning a different piano chord pulled me out the bed. I reached over to her empty side of the bed and grabbed a pillow to pin over my head. The cover was flung from off my body. I tossed the pillow aside and gave her a hateful gaze.

Carla was this beautiful, brown skinned thing that I called my wife. There weren't too many women in Detroit that were finer than her. Hell, maybe only Thelma from Good Times caught my eye more. Waking up to a beautiful face puts your soul at ease. You'd think a man would have nothing to complain about, right? Her teeth were as white as the Beatles. She flashed them at me. I groaned and put the pillow back over my face.

"Dom, get up," she said.

I had a long night and wasn't in the mood.

"Dom, get up and go wake up Tasha."

"You can't wake her up?"

"You done turned her against me. I damn near got to break her arm to get her to listen."

I sat up and reached to my nightstand and grabbed one of many glasses of water and downed it. I yanked the night light out of the plug and left it on the floor. I got out of the bed and slid my feet across the hardwood floors. My lifeless body bounced off the cheap grain wood paneling from wall to wall. Photos of dead family members watched me as I slithered through the long hall. Tasha's room was at the end of the hall on the left. I turned to the door and the family dog laid at the foot of her bed.

His floppy ears perked up when he saw me walk in. He stood up slow and stretched before walking over to me. I rubbed his head and sent him out of the room. A buddy of mine owned a farm and sold him to me for ten dollars. He was a jet-black Labrador named Muddy and man did he cry and wail the whole way home. I told Tasha how he sounded like Muddy Waters and the name stuck. There wasn't a place that Tasha went, that he wasn't too far behind.

Her lava lamp gave the room a purple hue until I opened the blinds. I kicked an unsolved Rubik's cube over towards another unnecessary toy, that damn Easy Bake Oven. I can't remember ever having a toy growing up. We would just run around outside. We'd shoot each other with our fingers playing cowboys and Indians or climb trees and almost put our eyes out throwing rocks at each other.

When I was young, we moved over to the North End of Detroit. Pop started working at a Ford Plant and mom worked for some white folks named the Jeffersons. Apparently, that was one of the best jobs a Negro could get back then. If you worked for white folks, everybody thought you made it.

White folks don't mind Negroes having money, long as they get it from other white folks. My grandpop had his own business and money. All the time, he'd be running stuff to and from Canada. Illegal stuff I assume. Naturally, he caught hell from them white folks. So much he even had to close his legitimate stores.

I remember how we used to go to the corner store and buy them big pickles that were damn near the size of a mortar. We'd get to a rooftop and wait. Me, Kenny Red and another brother named Baby Chuck. With our backs against the rooftop ledge we listened below. Footsteps. We'd always hear that same voice. "Good morning" he'd say to Mrs. Pearlman who owned the laundromat.

We had our target. Officer Patterson. We'd jump up and rocket those pickles at him. They were so heavy that they nearly knocked him off his feet. By the time he realized what hit him, we'd be long gone.

I don't know how he never caught us. He had to of known it was us. That's what we did for fun. Now these kids are kind of far out. Tasha had asked me for a pet rock. That was it, a rock that you could buy. I couldn't believe it. I yelled at her and told her to go outside and get one.

I plopped down on her bed and shook her little body.

"Come on baby girl, you know what time it is."

She threw a pillow over her head.

"Aww, can I stay home?"

"Uh, no."

"I'm sick," she said with some lazy cough. I stared through her. She knew I wasn't going for it. "When I grow up, I'm gonna have a job like you so I don't have to work."

7

"What? I go to work early and stay late every day."

"Mama says you just sit around and argue with people."

"Girl your mama don't know what she's talking about."

I tickled her and hit her over the head with the pillow. She flashed a little snagtooth smile and jumped on me. Muddy had been lying at the door. He ran back inside thinking it was play time. I put an end to that and stood up and told her to get ready for school. On my way out her room I grabbed a bow that was on the floor.

"Don't forget to wear your bow today."

She groaned.

"But I don't want to. I always lose it. Plus, red isn't my favorite color."

"Wear it. It's pretty," I said as I went back to my room and got ready for the day.

Fifteen minutes later I said goodbye to the girls and walked out the front door. We lived in the Boston-Edison District where Henry Ford, Berry Gordy and Joe Louis all once lived. The district, with its huge, sturdy homes was built in the early 1900s. Each home was built in a unique way, from relatively small homes like ours, to huge mansions.

We bought the house from an older white couple a few years earlier with $20,000 that I got from my VA loan. The husband said he had every plan on staying in Detroit. He had lived here all his life. But the Riots of 1967 started just three blocks away and that was too close for comfort. He and his wife left as soon as they found a buyer.

The house next to ours was owned by the Oldhams. Carla used to force me to spend time with them a few years back. Those play dates stopped when they called us "uppity". I guess two parents working and driving two cars was a bad thing.

To be fair, it wasn't usual. Carla drove a '75 Cadillac and I was pushing a '73 Dodge Challenger. Man did that thing make a mean growl through the streets.

I drove south on 12th street, pass where the riots had started nine years earlier. Them were days that I'll never forget. They act like Negroes were just running wild for no reason but that's not true.

They had thrown up freeways in the middle of the prosperous Negro neighborhoods. So we began to spread out over the city. We moved the Negro business section to 12th street. Isn't it funny how wherever Negroes thrive, there is always a "riot" or something to burn the shit up? Watts, Rosewood, Newark. White folks can't stand to see Negroes doing well for themselves.

I hadn't been back in the states for more than a month. We got word about a party for some other soldiers that were coming home from Vietnam. Old Bill Scott was the host of the festivities. He was a local politician of some sort. Also a certified hustler. He would host parties at this old Economy Printing building. The problem was, Bill didn't have a liquor license so he always got raided.

The thing about it, was the police had to see criminal activity with their own eyes. They can't just say some illegal shit was going on. We were in there grooving. Drenched in sweat. It had to be 120 degrees inside. The story goes some guy walked in and bought a beer. Bill didn't know it, but he was a cop.

As soon as he slid the money across the bar, the front door was kicked in. People flew everywhere. Women screaming, men wrestling around. The city went up in flames after that. The rest is history.

Negro frustration was at an all-time high. Kicked around by

the police squad called the big four. Trapped in ghettos like rats and not to mention the heat. Man was it hot outside. Not just the flames, but it was in the middle of July. Something about the heat makes a man lose his senses.

I won't say much about my actions during the riot. I put my life on the line for this country. When I came back, I began to see the world different. I was pissed off with a huge chip on my shoulder. You do the math.

People everywhere, running in and out of shops and businesses. Kids tossing bricks through windows. It was white folks doing it too. I was up on the roof with a rifle in hand. I see this elderly white woman coming out of a clothing store. She had just received a huge discount on some merchandise. She slipped away into the crowd undetected by the camera. They kept that to themselves, it was easier to blame a Negro.

I saw something I'll never forget. I was looking at one store when movement at another caught me. I saw the flaming bottle crash into a store. What is so strange about it was that it was a white boy throwing it. I took a shot but missed. He disappeared into the alley.

I can't lie, a part of me liked the burning we did. The old man that I shot? Well we sent the whole village up in flames anyway. Schultz was so giddy that he looked to be dancing in the blaze. I thought him the craziest son of a bitch I had ever met when I saw that. Then I noticed myself doing the same outside an electronics repair shop. The white folks were dead set on mistreating us. And we were dead set against it. That scene was burned in my mind.

The gun shots made me feel alive. It was like being back in Vietnam. Once a soldier goes into war mode, it's nearly impossible to get out of it. He's always on edge. Always trying to find the quickest way out of a room if need be. Always sizing a man up. A country needs its soldiers to think that way, trust me.

That morning, no lit bottles were being thrown. There were no snipers on the roofs. But the city was still a war zone. No tanks rode through the streets as traffic flowed on Jefferson Ave.

I strolled by where they were building the Renaissance Center. A huge complex of buildings that towered in the sky. It was strange seeing something like that being built. The irony couldn't be missed. It was a beacon of hope for a city that had been called the "murder capital of the world" just two years before. I hate to admit it, but all those reports were true.

I had been in court the week prior for a murder trial. There was a white family that had a gathering on the east side. One of the uncles did what uncles do. Sit around, drink and talk shit. He had been punking his niece's husband. Jokes, punching him in the arm, general disrespect.

The boyfriend was a real hot head. He hid it well for the better part of four months but all that pressure built up in him. That day he pulled out a .357 Magnum and let off five rounds. Everyone was in the house. Aunts, uncles, grandmas. He chased that old boy out the back door, shooting the whole time.

The uncle died faced down in the backyard. There goes Fourth of July for them. But here's the worst part. The man's defense said that because he was a veteran of the Korean War, he suffers from something called "gross stress reaction". I had never heard of it. They said it's a pattern of reaction that deals with overwhelming fear or some shit like that.

He killed a man in cold blood, and they were trying to say that he did it because he had been a soldier. As a soldier, you know exactly what the hell you're doing. That's what makes you a soldier. How do you make sense of shit like that? That's the garbage we would see on a daily. He could've just fought the uncle hand to hand. This city makes me feel sick sometimes.

There's an island in Detroit called Belle Isle. It's named after some little white girl. It's smack dab in the middle of the sparkling Detroit River between us and Canada. It's a groovy little place that offers an escape from the concrete jungle. For all the bullshit we went through, we had some cool things too.

I parked the car in a lot that overlooked the river. An elderly couple walked in matching track suits behind me. It was crazy to think that the riot of 1943 started on this island. If I had any super power in the world, it would've been to look back in the past. I sat still and tried to visualize how shit looked back in the day.

Negroes coming up north from the south. From Alabama, Georgia, Tennessee to Detroit, Chicago & Philly. Cars loaded up with everything they own. Everybody wearing dresses and suits. Hats and suspenders. All running from the hatred that is the Jim Crow south.

But when they get here, they realized they had been duped and that the North wasn't much better. Them Northern whites didn't want to see Negroes in chains, that's true. But in fact, they don't want to see them at all. All the Negroes were packaged in these ramshackle neighborhoods called Black Bottom and Paradise Valley. All that racial tension began to build up. I closed my eyes and the image of a brother punching a racist white boy made me smile.

When I opened them again I was back in my time. Across the River, new construction continuously changed the sky line of the murder capital. With all the vacancies, crime and people fleeing the city, somebody was still making some good dough here.

What had been there before they started building? Warehouses? Slaughterhouses? My childhood neighborhood was in the midst of it all and I couldn't remember what was there. Isn't it funny how you can pass something every day and not really know what you're looking at? Or maybe my memory was getting bad. Sometimes I felt older than I actually was.

3

Chapter 3

Merle might have been a construction worker in her youth. From the beaten leathery skin to her rough hands. She was fifty but didn't look a day younger than eighty. Rumor had it that when she was born, the doctor gave her a cigarette to quiet her and she hasn't put them down since. When she spoke, it was easy to forget that a woman was talking. She was a nice old lady though. Sweet, helpful, but not too easy on the eyes. But this new girl that had been hired was a stone cold fox. I had heard about her before I saw her and those words didn't do her any justice.

I love Carla but this girl gave her a run for her money. Her name was Michelle Allen. In any other life, she could've been a Jet Beauty of the Week. I mean the woman was stacked. Five foot three. A smile that could make a dead man blush, and thighs like a horse. She drove them white boys crazy so imagine what she did to me.

The mayor began an initiative to hire more Negroes in the force to reflect the city. It was normal that at any office you'd go into, a Negro woman was right at the front door. They would show them off and say "look, we are diverse" while photos of all white officers were behind her.

Every morning I stood at the glass doors and made sure my hair was nice and brushed. I'd slick down my eyebrows and enter the building. Some of the white officers would speak as I made my way up to the third floor. Some of them didn't. It didn't bother me either way. I always looked forward to hearing "Hey Mr. Detective" from Chelle.

I was drawn to her desk. I couldn't help it. I'd make up excuses to stop and talk to her. At least twice a week for the last five months she had been there, we'd go out to lunch. Talking to her just felt normal. She had me open without even trying. That day we were talking gardening.

"Try putting some of the pots you have into bowls that have a little water in them," she said. I leaned in closer on her desk. The cinnamon aroma filled my nose. "That way the plant won't take on any more water than it needs."

"Yeah? I gotta try that come next spring. What do you grow?"

"Not a lot. My backyard ain't too big but I had some real good tomatoes this year, a couple cucumbers too."

"Well I need your help because everything that I touch has been dying lately."

"What do you mean lately?"

"Well, pretty much ever since I got back from the Marines. Now it's like everything refuses to grow."

"Well, uh, why do you think?"

"You the expert, you tell me."

She opened her mouth to speak and then closed it suddenly. I spoke.

"What?"

"Well, I don't know how to say it."

15

"Say what?"

"Well, my mama always says that plants are real smart and feed off you."

"Are you gonna keep talking in riddles?"

"I just. The plant reflects the planter, okay?"

I stared at her for a moment. I could tell she was nervous. I was told I had an intimidating presence.

"You need to speak life to it, you know? You gotta plant them with some love."

"I ain't doing anything no different than what my mama used to do."

"Well you're doing something different cause you can't grow shit. My mama don't say too much that's wrong," she shrugged her narrow shoulders.

"Where is she from?"

"Alabama. If it come out the ground, she can tell you all about it. And if it walks on four legs, my daddy can catch it."

"Your pop sounds like he'd be my man. What part of Alabama?"

"Outside of Birmingham. Poor daddy, he wanted a boy so bad and ended up with five loud mouth girls. We still drive him crazy.

"God, I can't imagine no shit like that. Tasha's more than enough for me to handle."

"How is your little boss?"

"Growing too fast. I wish she would just stay this little forever."

"It's so cute that she's your weakness."

"Weakness?"

I didn't have any weakness. I was built strong and solid. Never bent and never folded. They didn't make them like me

16

anymore.

"Yep. You this tall, strong brother that can kill a lion but when it comes to her, you turn to mush. It's ok, my daddy is the same way."

"Well I wouldn't call that a weakness."

"Ok, how about a soft spot?"

"I mean, you know, I gotta protect my baby."

"I bet Carla loves that. How is she?"

"She's cool. We had a little family date yesterday."

She flashed that bright smile again. God damn was she gorgeous. Some son of a bitch sure was lucky. She told me she had dated some wanna be Black Panther before but nothing really came of it. I continued.

"Yeah, we brought Muddy with us down to Belle Isle. He finally learned how to play fetch. Between the two of them, I barely had enough energy to come in today."

"She is so adorable. I bet her and Kathryn would get along so well."

"You have a daughter?" I asked.

She cut her brown eyes at me.

"Dominique, whatever your middle name is Broddie, I done told you about my little girl at least two times now. She's five."

"Oh ok, yeah, yea, I remember now. You told me because you uh, went to her little school thing. How is she?"

I doubt she believed me. I wouldn't have. Did she actually tell me about her? I would've remembered. I'm not a selfish person.

She told me some story about how her daughter beat up a boy in class for making fun of her or something like that. I tend to zone out when I'm talking to people. It's not on purpose, my mind just wanders. When I came to she had mentioned Carla.

17

"Since we're talking about her, let me ask you something," I said.

"Okay, what?"

"Are you the romantic type?"

"Yes."

"Well Carla is," I said, jumping the gun. I thought her answer would have been different.

"She likes to hold hands in public and kiss and all that bullshit."

"I think every woman does."

"But that's the problem to me, that isn't real love."

"What do you mean 'real love'?"

I took a breath.

"Real love is me protecting her. Like when I almost killed a guy on Jefferson a few weeks ago."

"Oh my God Dom, you almost did what?"

"We were all out getting ice cream. I was in the bathroom and heard the damn dog barking up a storm. So I ran outside and see some fucking wino right next to Carla's window. He's saying something to her. And-"

"What was he saying?"

"At the time I couldn't hear anything. It all went silent and I was seeing red. Carla said he was going off on her about not giving him any money."

"She's a fighter isn't she?"

"Through and through. I don't remember it but said I ran over to him full speed. I grabbed him by his collar and tossed him fifteen feet to the building. He started pleading for his life. She said I had this look in my eye that scared her."

"I bet you did. Did he leave it alone after that?"

"He didn't have any choice after I hit him and broke his jaw."

Behind us, the only other Negro detective walked in. An old timer named Wendell Wright. His head almost hit the ceiling. Calm and collected. Could beat up any man in his youth. Never lost his cool, not even once. Real life Ron O'Neal type. The building could be on fire and he'd be the last one to emerge. On his way out the door, he'd stop and use the flames to light his cigarette. He was everything I wanted to be with this job.

I slapped his hand and he greeted Chelle before going off to his desk. Chelle and I continued.

"So what happened next? she asked. She propped up on her elbows and stared into my eyes. She always made me feel like I was heard.

"I was foaming at the mouth as she and some of the men around pulled me off the guy."

"Dom," she said as she covered her face with her palms. "Don't go out and kill people. I mean, it's good for a woman to know that her man has her back but sometimes we just want a man to rub our backs. You know, make us feel secure in other ways. Do you compliment her?"

"On what?"

"You know, like how she looks, smells, her hair even."

"She got girl friends for all that."

We spent the next twenty minutes going back and forth. According to her, women like all that shit from the movies. You know, putting a coat over a puddle and kicking cans down the street. It's all bullshit to me. I'm a protector. Plain and simple. That's where my love comes from.

She didn't seem to understand it. I didn't expect her too. I won't lie, I cut her off many times during the conversation. I already knew what she was going to say. All women say the same things really. But if women want to be equal, then we need to have real equality. Not just when it's convenient. She threw her hands up in frustration and scolded me.

"Well, I can tell you one of her biggest problems with you and she and I have never even met."

"And what's that?"

"She doesn't get a chance to talk," she said, the frustration clear in her tone. "Even if what you're saying is right, you don't let her get a word in."

"Bull, she says more than enough."

I noticed that my jaw clenched and my defenses rose. I needed reinforcements. I leaned from her desk and looked for Wendell.

"Hey Dell, what do you do when your wife tries to hold your hand and all that extra jive?"

He looked up at me in the open workspace. Cubicles hadn't taken hold yet.

"You really wanna know Dom?" he asked in that cool voice of his.

"Yeah, I asked didn't I? You're an old school brother. What would you do?"

I looked down at Carla and mouthed, "Watch this".

"I would shut my mouth and hold my wife's hand," he smiled.

"See?" said Chelle. "You gotta be able to give in sometimes. Even a strong bridge has to be able to bend or else it's gonna crumble."

"Oh I didn't know you were an engineer. Did you-"

The aroma of cheap cigarettes hit my nose and ruined the party. My nose burning meant that my partner George Syman-ski had heard enough of the Negro fun. He always seemed to be bothered by Negroes laughing. If a group of us were just enjoying ourselves in public, he'd be the one to come around and ask "What's going on here?"

On short stubby legs, he lurked down the aisle. His stomach bulged from his tucked in green shirt. His glory days were gone but he must've been some athlete in his younger days. He sounded like he was gasping for air with every word he spoke.

"Good morning Broddie, thanks for coming in today. I hate to break up the 'get down' but we got a case we need to head out to. Lieutenant Mitchells says it's pretty serious."

4

Chapter 4

I don't know who said that opposites attract, but he was a stone-cold liar. I wish he could have sat in the back seat of the car. I was in the passenger seat next to my exact opposite and I could've name 45 places that I would have rather been. From the first day I met him, I knew we weren't going to get along.

He had two strikes against him. One, he was white. I was born just a few years after the race riot of '43 so my skepticism of whites was warranted. The second strike was that he called me a "soul brother" when we had just met. And no, not in a cool, hip way. There was no going back for him at that point. He might have had ten years old me. Too old and too white to be anyone's "soul brother".

Woodward Avenue served as the divider between the east and west sides of the city. The theme song to the Jeffersons said they were 'moving on up, to the east side'. That always made me laugh because it was the exact opposite in my city.

Detroit owed its growth and success to one thing and one thing only. The auto industry. When that started to decline in the fifties, the white folks started leaving the city. Twenty years later we started to see the effects of losing that much of a tax base.

Negroes were itching to leave the infested ghettos we were locked in. Corrupt agencies sold the vacant homes to Negroes at prices sometimes double what they were actually worth. Negroes usually have unreliable employment due to racist hiring and they too began to lose their homes. This turned Detroit into the place that it is now known for. Vacant neighborhoods. Crime among the youth. It's a domino effect.

George Symanski always had a way of ruining my peace. Whether I was talking to Chelle or just thinking, he always jumped in and disturbed me.

Years of tobacco abuse had beaten his voice. When I first heard him cough, I thought he had TB. There was one good thing about me meeting him. I stopped smoking cold turkey. I try not to learn the hard way.

"Two officers shot, now why doesn't that surprise me?" he said.

"It seems to be happening often."

"So often that they're even shooting at Negro cops now. You gotta be just as careful as me you know?" he laughed.

It wasn't funny so I didn't laugh. I wasn't a favorite around the precinct. Maybe that was the reason. Richard Higgins was a Negro detective in another precinct. All day his huge teeth were on display. He smiled and chuckled with them white folk. Now he was uppity. One of them bougie, high yellow niggas that always talked about his physician father and tried to impress them. He was one of the biggest ass kissers I had ever met, of course they loved him.

"Awh come on," Symanski said. "You gotta lighten up in this line of work."

"I'm light enough."

"Like hell you are. You know, my daddy had a friend named Chuck Simmons. Chuck was one of the first men in the FBI you know? He spent all his time studying crazies. He was so into his work that he never even once took the time to vacation and laugh."

I faced the window. The early morning sun shined. Maybe I could have walked the rest of the way. Symanski continued.

"When he was in town, him and dad sat up for hours, trading stories. He was a depressed old coot. He survived shootouts, fights with the fucking mafia, car chases, explosions, the whole nine. And you know what took him out?"

"No," I said stoically.

"Fucking cancer, can you believe that? Cancer. I think it came from him not learning to lighten up. That shit is bad for you kid. You won't catch me stressed out about any of it. No sir."

He took a long puff of his cigar and then blew out. The smoke was vacuumed out the car by the cracked window.

"A cop shot in the face is actually light work you know?" he said.

"How?" He had my interest now.

"Awh hell, God damn Barney Fife could give you a motive for this without ever leaving the TV screen. We got a couple young Negro motorists that were pulled over by some cops. Neither side trusts the other and they all got their fingers on the triggers the whole time. Both sides made a sudden move that the other didn't trust. The cops didn't do a thorough survey of the situation and boom. There's your motive. I've done my job, I can go home for the day."

"But that's not a motive. A motive is a reason."

"What else do you need?"

"That just explains what happens," I said.

"Negro motorists who think they are treated bad so they lash out the best way they know how."

"What do you mean think?"

"Things aren't how they used to be Broddie. We go out of our way to make Negroes feel comfortable."

"What? Things are exactly how they used to be."

"Oh no, in my daddy's day they...well, things have gotten better, Broddie. Look enough of all that negative shit, we got a golden ticket with this case."

"What do you mean a golden ticket?"

"It's from Willy Wonka and the-"

"I know who the fuck Willy Wonka is. I mean how is it a golden ticket? Jesus Christ."

"That boy that got his face blown off? He was one of the mayor's 'golden boys'. Word around the precinct is that he was like his nephew or some shit."

"So, if we solve it the mayor likes us?" I asked.

"Bingo buddy boy. You know the process when a cop gets killed. It's almost personal. It always goes up to the mayor's office."

"If we track down the sons of bitches who did this-"

"Exactly. We're looking at some big time promotions buddy boy. Hell, maybe even a medal from the mayor."

That stirred something in me. I used to watch how men feared and revered the top brass in the Marine Corps. I wanted to be those men. A leader. An air of power around me that would let me move men with the swing of a hand. I had tossed that in the back of my mind for nearly a decade. I began to feel alive again.

When I first got back to the States I instantly went through the motions. The days were quick. The nights everlasting. The bright poinsettias turned dull and bland. Even mom's macaroni lost its flavor. I was only twenty-one at the time but I felt sixty-one.

Those past ten years had been much of the same. But that morning in Symanski's car, the orange and yellow leaves stood out to me again. That ambition made me feel alive again. It was like I had been brought back to life. I stared out the window. My mind drifted to the jungle and how it changed me.

We were the last ones on the scene. I guess the whole city got the memo before us. Or maybe the small traces of black smoke pulled them over. Someone or something had been set on fire. I braced myself for what we'd find.

A horde of people blocked the intersection of Van Dyke & Six Mile. Years before this had been a mostly Polish area. As they began to flee for the suburbs, Negroes moved in. They all stretched their necks over one another to get a glimpse of the carnage.

Our officers had completely blocked off the five lanes of traffic on Van Dyke. We parked and approached the mass of onlookers. Symanski looked at me and asked if I would be alright. I didn't do well with crowds but I assured him that I would. I tossed my badge in the air and yelled out "Pardon me, Detective here" repeatedly.

Halfway through the crowd, my lungs began to tighten. The faces in the crowd began to melt. I thought to myself, "Had it been that hot a few minutes ago?" I swallowed and pushed through the group almost ready to faint. My knees wobbled. I was sure that I would fall and be trampled. Just as I began to go down and scream, I burst through to the front. I took a deep breath and wiped the sweat off my forehead. Symanski looked at me.

"That shit isn't normal. You ought to get it checked out."

I scoffed at him. "I'm fine."

A bare faced cop from our precinct walked over to me. Young and scared as a rabbit in a bear's den, Jamie Simons was a cool young cat. Eager to make things better, he always meant well. His face lit up when he saw us.

"Boy am I glad to see you two. Say, are you alright Dom?"

He shook our hands.

"Yeah, I'm fine."

"These folks are crazy out here. I almost had to poke a few with my stick."

"Are you the responding officer?" Symanski asked, cutting through all the bull.

"Oh, yes sir, come follow me but brace yourselves, this ain't pretty."

"Is anything around here?" said Symanski. I'd never admit it out loud, but I had begun to agree with him on that point.

Jamie motioned for another officer to take his place at the front of the crowd and we went towards the fiery commotion. I had trouble keeping up with his long stride and I know ole stubby legged Symanski did too. Jamie looked back at us and spoke in a boisterous voice.

He gave us the run down. Officers Keanan Lyles and Nelson Cooke were minding their own business. A car flew by them and didn't care who saw. It swerved in and out of traffic. For whatever reason, it stopped. Lyles and Cooke approached and an hour later, we showed up. In the middle of his briefing, a loud flash grabbed my attention.

Photographers and reporters were the absolute worst. Slimy,

slippery bastards that will do anything to get their name attached to something. Eric McNamara had managed to weasel his way into our crime scene. He must have shit Irish bricks when he saw us come towards him. His little voice cracked.

"Hey, hey, good morning gentlemen, I, I was just leaving."

"Hand it over," Symanski barked at him.

"It doesn't even have any film. Damn it, I always do this."

Symanski snatched the camera and opened the film roll. He yanked it out and tossed the film on the asphalt. Eric's eyes dulled as Symanski gifted the empty camera back to him. I was hoping he would have kicked it but instead he gave him a lecture.

"We haven't even notified the man's family and you're already taking pictures of him?"

"Well, I, I..." Eric stuttered. I balled my fist tight. Symanski continued his scolding.

"Where is the God damn decency? Get the fuck out of here. Eric you know better."

Eric's shoulders slumped down to the pavement.

"If I catch you around another of my scenes it's gonna be more than your film that gets tossed."

George Symanski was old school. He practiced racism, sexism and bigotry, all by the book. Those three things began to become unpopular at the time, but he was a man who said what he meant and meant what he said. I respected at least that part about him. I'd rather know who I'm dealing with than him smile in my face with fake bullshit.

Like a wounded cat, Eric scurried out of the crime scene, back to the alley he came from. I refused to let Symanski out do me. I looked over at the officers who stood the front line.

"Hey," I yelled out.

"Yeah?" a big burly brother said.

"What's that yellow tape say?"

He turned to read it the "Police line do not cross" out loud to me. I felt like a grade school teacher. Sure, I was a detective, but half of my job was dealing with grown children. I stared at him for a few seconds.

"Well if they don't have a fucking badge, don't let them cross it, Jesus Christ."

Symanski turned back to Jamie.

"Please, continue."

"Yes, uh well, like I was saying, what you see over there, is what became of poor Lyles."

I crept toward the soulless body. He was laid out on his back, just how they left him. The side of his face that received the shotgun blast faced the sun. Chunks of his mustached face were blown into the median lane. It was the most gruesome scene I had seen on the job.

I crouched down to get a good look at his head. Small pieces of skull were mixed in with black powder and brain tissue. It reminded me of Private Everett. We had been a part of the scout team in Vietnam. We went around with dogs and all that to look for the VC.

We were picking through the thicket. Drenched in sweat. Swarmed by bugs baked at three hundred and fifty degrees. Sticks of bamboo were taller than any building we had seen outside of Saigon. It was around six in the afternoon. Light wasn't an issue until we went further in the jungle.

Jason was out in front, he was just that kind of guy. Strong, dependable, a fighter. He had to be just as scared as I was. With one wrong step your life could've been over. Or even worse, you lose a leg and end up living and wishing you were dead.

Jason suddenly stopped. I could just make out his outline. He threw up his fist and crouched. Silence. The entire world stopped. Either a tear or a bead of sweat raced down my chin. Jason turned his head to his left. He took one step and bam. The ground opened up under him. Dirt flew everywhere.

When I came to, I heard a loud ringing. Muffled bullets zipped just inches over my head. I scrambled for my rifle and crawled. I looked back and I wished I hadn't. Jason's legs were both gone. His head looked much like Officer Lyles'.

I can make sense of it in Vietnam. They're God damn Communists. But this was America, not some thicket outside Saigon. Lyles laid in the street looking at the sky. At least he had both his legs.

I stared at him and mustered the strength to speak.

"They shot him from about six feet away with a hmm, Remington Model 870, looks like," I told Symanski.

"Jesus, Dom, how the fuck can you get so close to that?"

Symanski threw his hands over his stomach. I looked over at the fire boys that were still on the scene. Two of them held the hose and vanquished the remaining embers that engulfed the police cruiser. A pile of smoldering metal billowed black smoke into the fall air.

"Hey Symanski, you bring marsh mellows? What's the story with that?" I asked Officer Simons. Sweat ran down from under my turtle neck.

"We're dealing with some pretty fucked up young cats Dom, I mean Detective Broddie. After they shoot them, they tossed a fire bomb at the car."

"What do you think Symanski? Making a political state-ment?"

"Nah, don't look too political to me."

"Then what?"

"They're teenagers. Nothing makes sense. So Simons, let me get this straight."

Symanski blew out smoke.

"I've got a car full of four young Negroes joyriding around until they are pursued by Officers Keanan Lyles and Nelson Cooke. So far so good?"

"Spot on," Simons replied.

"Of course I am. They continue to chase until they come to rest here at the intersection. The two arresting officers approach the vehicle and immediately take heavy fire from the occupants."

"Yes sir."

"Lyles loses his face while Cooke is wounded. The Negroes then exit the vehicle and light a bonfire before leaving the crime scene."

"Right again sir," Simons said.

"And what in the way of suspects?"

"Four young, perhaps teenaged Negroes."

Symanski dropped his notepad at his side.

"Don't jerk me around Simons, I know that. I've got one hundred and fifty teenage Negroes out here right now. Should I go round every one of them up?"

"Well no sir I–"

"Exactly because we would need more men. What did they look like? Because from what you're telling me, you think that all Negroes look alike and that's just fucking insensitive."

Simons couldn't hide the red flustering in his high yellow face. Symanski spoke for him.

"Let me take a wild guess. Huge afros with a pick sticking out the backing. Black leather jackets and some sunglasses?"

"No suspect description, sir."

"Detective Broddie, I don't know about you but I see about six hundred faces out here. Simons, are you telling me that not one gave you a description?"

Simons had been looking down. I guess he had been hoping I would jump in and save him. Now he looked up into Symanski's eyes.

"Well, with all due respect, that's your job. You come here to detect, Detective and put together what I don't get paid to see."

If I could've hugged Simons right then and there, I would've. It was like a big brother watching his younger brother finally stand up to the neighborhood bully. Symanski had a scowl on his crusted mug. Oh how that made my day. He pulled out another cigarette and suggested we start to talk to the crowd.

The most difficult part of our job was community outreach. Here we are putting our lives on the line every day. We risked it all to protect the community. And when we go to talk to the community about protecting it, we got cold shoulders. I had so many doors slammed in my face that I stopped counting after the first week. I can't blame the people though. Hell, the police force was made to keep Negroes in check in this country.

I had a rule when looking for witnesses. I avoided talking to any males under thirty-five unless they were the last option. I always started with the women. They were more sympathetic to crime. Usually they could picture their loved one in the victim's position and helped you out. I zeroed in on one in particular who held a sleeping child on her shoulder.

I walked towards her and before I could get my name out, she walked away from me. This went on for another thirty minutes until a familiar voice called out to me. The trouble making face was older than the last time I saw him, but his voice had stayed the same. High pitched and spotty. I spoke to him.

"Johnnie C. Parlor, how's everything in your world young brother?"

He glared at me.

"You know, still poor, still black."

"Yeah, I feel you brother."

"Do you?" The little shit scrunched his face at me. I wondered why you stopped chasing us around. What? You got tired of being around the ghetto? Too many of us?"

"Man cut that bullshit. If anything, there's more Negroes where I'm working now."

"Where? Watching over them white folks in Greektown?"

"Nope. Over near West Grand and the Lodge. You should come down there some day. I'd love to see you there," I grinned at him.

Johnnie was a teenager. For all the shit we gave each other when he was younger, I actually liked him. He was a smart young cat. Well spoken. Strong willed. He was just misguided. We'd often trade jabs at each other but nothing too serious.

Nobody under the age of twenty-one was allowed to get under my skin. I was too well trained to lose my cool. I had met too many vicious men. Hell, when I was his age, I was preparing my mind to go to boot camp the following year.

"I bet you would," he replied. "You'd give your left nut to see another young brother locked up."

"The only people I want to see locked up are the ones who killed a fellow officer who was doing his best to protect little motherfuckers like you."

"We don't need your protecting. The Panthers patrolled their own neighborhoods. We can handle ourselves."

His crew behind him shook their heads in agreement as he went on.

"What we can't handle is some pig breathing down our asses every day while them white boys do the same things and walk away easy. Look, maybe it's a reason them brothers blasted at those pigs."

"So, it was a group of brothers?"

"Hey, I didn't see anything Jack."

He tossed his hands in the air and backed up.

"Well you see that pig over there?" I pointed to a white sheet that covered Officer Lyles' body. "That pig got his face blown off and happened to be a friend of mine. That's somebody's son, dad, brother, not a fucking pig. So, unless you're going to give me some information, I suggest you get the fuck out the way."

My rage softened his face and now he looked every bit of eighteen. He stood up straight and fixed his leather jacket and lightly patted his huge Afro that bounced every time he shook his head.

"Alright, look Jack, I didn't see shit. And, I, I guess I feel for the brother that lost his life. Pig or not, he was still a brother, just a little misguided."

Maybe he wasn't so bad after all. Perhaps these years had taught him something. I let him continue.

"I wish they had finished off the white boy instead. While I didn't see shit, it don't mean that I don't know shit, you dig?"

"I'm listening," I said.

"It was a car full of young cats who ain't got nothing on they mind but murder. They all Negroes, two dark and the other two real light. One kinda looked like Donald Goines, maybe he was a mulatto."

I scribbled on my pad as quick as I could.

"Have you ever seen them around here before?"

He looked around and leaned in closer to me.

"Look, you ain't hear this from me, okay, but one of them stays with his daddy at a junkyard not too far from here."

"Really? Where?"

"That I don't know, but I do know his mama died and he got this real big mustache that covers his whole face."

"How tall is he?"

"He's a pretty big guy. I'd say six-one, six-two maybe. His daddy's a funny little motherfucker, always joking. He ain't gone find this one too funny."

"What's his name?"

"His name is Lamont and his daddy's name is Fred. His nickname for him is, 'you big dummy!'"

I don't embarrass easy but he found a way to get to me that day. He must have planned that since I last saw him. He grabbed onto the punks around him for support. They hooped and hollered so loud that all of Van Dyke from Six Mile down to Gratiot could hear him. After he wiped his eyes, he gave me a cold stare.

"You think I'm gonna tell a fucking pig anything? Your boy got what he asked for. I ain't see shit 'Detective' and if I did, I wouldn't tell you."

Usually I'm a very calm and collected cat. I had just patted myself on the back saying how no one under twenty one could get to me. Well that was the closet I had ever been to strangling someone at the crime scene whose name wasn't George Symanski.

I was seconds away from being front page news. I had every intention of stomping him and handcuffing him and seeing if he was laughing then. Luckily something caught my eye. I turned back to him.

"You went and fucked up now," I said as I walked away.

A small group had gathered around a false prophet. Symanski stood in front of the man listening to his every word. He didn't know me, but I was very familiar with him.

His name was Reverend Brown and our beef had gone back for several years. Now, we never had officially met but we still had some history together. Standing on either side of him was a hungry looking Negro and some far out, space cadet looking white boy. Together they looked like some funky Holy Trinity.

Symanski was in for an hour of pure bullshit, I knew that much. He was busy jotting things down when I put my hand on his shoulder.

"What's this?" I asked.

"This pastor claims to be one of the leaders out here."

"He ain't no leader."

"But he's the only one around that makes even half a bit of sense. I'm gonna interview him when-"

"That's a waste of yours and my time."

"I think you got this guy pegged all wrong Broddie. He don't seem so bad. How do you mean?"

"That's Reverend Brown. You gone get an ear full of hot air coming from him. Let's roll. We need to go see Officer Cooke."

5

Chapter 5

The Lodge Freeway separated Henry Ford Hospital from our precinct. You could probably stand on the roof of the precinct and break a window in the hospital with a stone. The posted speed limit was fifty-five but you'd be run over if you followed it. Symanski sped to the hospital nearly taking out several cars on the way.

When we walked into Cooke's room, Lieutenant Mitchells had been staring at the door. It was like he knew when we would arrive. I nodded at him. He excused himself from Cooke and his wife and walked out. Suddenly it became easier to breathe in the room.

Mitchells was a hard ass. Arrogant, loud mouthed. But he always managed to show some manners to women and the elderly. Them old folks always thought that showing respect to the elderly and women would somehow make them candidates to get into heaven. Meanwhile they had no problem disrespecting the rest of the world. His mustache covered all the skin from his nose to his lips. I would've given up a week's pay to see him without it.

Symanski and I introduced ourselves to Cooke's wife. She was nothing special. Exactly what you would expect for a man like Cooke. Floral pattern dress with cheap lipstick. I caught myself from the distraction. I turned to Nelson.

His eyes were sunken. Bandages were wrapped around his left shoulder.

"How are you Nelson?"

"I, I don't know how to answer that Dom." He didn't dare look at me. Even though his words were slow, he stumbled over them. He just stared down at his feet while his wife rubbed his left hand. Symanski spoke up.

"Well Nelson, rest easy. We're going to get them for what they did. Now, we aren't going to be in your hair too long. You know why we're here. Give us your account."

Nelson's story went completely as previously described. The only variation came with the actual shooting. It wasn't the driver and passenger who fired the shots. It was the two young men in the back.

"There were three Negroes in the car, maybe four. One of them talked like a Negro but he didn't much look like it. He might have been a mulatto. I didn't really get to study his face."

"Was he one of the shooters?" I asked.

"Yeah. As soon as we approached the car, the front windows rolled down. Keanan might've said five words to the driver when the back windows rolled down. If I hadn't turned at that last moment, I'd be-"

He cut himself short. Symanski continued.

"How old did they look?"

"Them two in the front were probably late teens, early twenties maybe. But the two in the back, they looked like fucking kids. Maybe sixteen."

"Can you give a good description on the four?" Symanski asked.

"They looked like typical Negroes," he said. Perhaps he forgot I was there. "The two in the front and the one who shot Keanan all had big Afros. The one that shot me just had a big mess of curly hair. Like he tried to have an Afro but his hair wouldn't hold it."

"Did you hear them say anything?"

"Yeah, the driver asked us 'What seems to be the problem?' real calm and then boom."

"And what kind of car were they in?"

"A brown Mercury Comet. I know that for sure. Rust was eating away at the bottom of it."

Cooke's hands shook as he spoke to us. The more he spoke, the more he began to ramble. We stopped him. It was better to give him time to compose himself. Besides, we now had enough information to begin an investigation.

We thanked him and his wife and began to walk towards the door. My foot was half out when he called us. He stared out the window at a rundown high-rise apartment building across the street.

"I think this is it for me, detectives."

Soft words of a quitter had always disgusted me. Immediately my hands began to shake and my foot tapped. I stopped myself.

"What do you mean?" Symanski asked.

"I'm fucking done here. This isn't police work."

"Take some time to think about it Cooke. Don't do anything rash, you know?" said Symanski. "We're going to-"

"Let me tell you a story," I cut in. I couldn't hold back any longer. "The first face I saw in Vietnam was Lieutenant Mason Kendall. A little white boy from Tampa Bay. What he lacked in height, he made up for in cruelty, as you'll see. He's driving me through the towns in this Jeep and explaining to me how things go there."

Cooke continued to stare at his feet.

"We get to base and I hop off the truck and meet Private Jason Everett. A white boy from some little hick town in Missouri. He's walking me to our barracks. We passed smiling men who wouldn't live to see the next week. Right in the center of the camp was an ornament. And you know what that was?"

"What?" Cooke finally looked up at me.

"Someone had cut off a human head and sat it on a post. And on the two posts next to it were the hands of that same soldier. I had never seen no shit like that. I just stared at it. Its eyes stared back at me. It cried for help and I wondered would the VC do the same to me. I tapped Jason on the shoulder and asked him about it."

Cooke's wife grabbed his hand even tighter. The story was making her uncomfortable.

"Jason said 'Why that's a human head' in a nonchalant tone. Lieutenant Kendall, that savage son of a bitch put out a call. He told his soldiers to bring him a head in exchange for some whiskey. A little extra if they brought back the hands."

I stared away at the apartment building he had been looking at and continued.

"It was some damn good whiskey too. You know what I learned from that?"

I turned back towards the pitiful man in front of me.

"No, I don't," Cooke said.

"Shit like that was in the job description. Maybe it was in the fine print, but when you go to war, you see some fucked up shit. And when you take an oath to protect people, you do so with your life."

I could've gone on and on. I didn't feel bad for him one bit. He was still alive. Besides, if a little bullet can knock you away from your purpose, you didn't belong here anyway. Good riddance.

I stepped out the door. To my right was the Lieutenant. His stonewall face startled me, but I didn't flinch. My nerves were pass that. He looked to be impressed with my little speech.

"Since I'm here, you might as well tell me what you got," he said.

Symanski spoke first.

"Sir, I think this was some kind of gang initiation. The two in the front seat were older. They weren't the shooters while two young ones in the back carried it out."

"So you think they took them out to do the shooting?"

"Yes sir. Looking for soft targets but then they get pulled over so they switch to the police."

"Sounds possible. What did any of the witnesses say?"

A young, gorgeous nurse walked by. She made eyes with me. I could see while I stared at the Lieutenant. I thought I had gotten real good at that. Mitchells cleared his throat.

"Are you with us Broddie?" the Lieutenant said.

"What was that, sir?"

"I said what did the witnesses say?"

"Uh, I, I was speaking to a few but they are not willing to talk. Maybe if we go back privately they will say something. They might not want to be seen talking to the police."

"I expected more of you Symanski," Mitchells said.

"Sir?"

"I partnered you with a young, hip, Negro detective for a reason. You had better learn to use what you have. The same goes for you," he pointed his fat trigger finger to me. "You two have direct insight into the community. We should have four Negroes in custody by now."

I knew by now that many of his conversations ended without a formal exit. He turned and went back into Cooke's room. Symanski and I walked off to the parking lot.

"Whatever happened to Jason?" Symanski asked. "You talk about him a lot."

"We got caught in an ambush."

"I know that but what happened?"

I didn't respond. When we got to the car, he asked again. I leaned on the trunk.

"We walked into a dark jungle looking for some VC. Jason is probably thirty feet in front of me.

"He was out in front of us with his dog. He stepped on a mine and triggered an ambush. He got shot up and riddled with bullets. We all hit the ground as bullets whizzed over our heads. When I came to, I saw him. He had seen better days. Our company was about as far back as that Buick back there."

I pointed to the red car.

"I didn't know it, but I'm running with an empty leash. One of them mines blew my dog Hendrix to bits. I look up and see trees with guns running at me. That's how out of it I was."

"Trees with guns?"

"Of course, they weren't trees with guns. They were camouflaged soldiers. Anyway, I ran back the way we came. Then something hit me. It felt like Hank Aaron hit me with a bat in the back of my leg. I can feel it now. I'm talking pain that makes you not speak straight."

I went around to his side of the car and pulled up my pants leg. I showed him the scar where a chunk had been taken out of my calf.

"Somehow I get up and run back to the company. I fell in their arms. The radio operator screamed. I can't hear it, but I see the veins in his neck popping. The air company couldn't find us in that thick jungle. You know what this kid did?"

"What?" Symanski added.

"He grabbed a canister of red smoke and ran like the wind. Ducking bullets the whole time. He lobbed the can at least five hundred feet. Once that smoke broke through the trees, it was over."

I looked up into the sky and could still see the plane swing over us.

"The napalm fell and turned everything in its path into a blaze. When I looked at them, the damn VC looked like they were doing a dance in the fire. You asked what happened to Jason. I sure do hope he was dead by the time that fire got to him. I'm sure his body turned back into the dust they say we come from.

That was the first time I told that story about Jason. He always told me to come visit him in Missouri. He had never met a Negro until he went to the Marines. I wondered if his people would trip if I visited his grave.

Symanski was floored. That wasn't the answer he was looking for. He changed the subject.

"Alright, well uh, let's go talk to some of the residents then."

"Right on, but first, let's make a little stop."

6

Chapter 6

I was always somewhat of a researcher. More like a historian if you will. Sometimes I would take my pop out for a drive around the city. I'd pick his brain and have him tell me how things used to be. He'd always sit me down and we'd stare at a map of Detroit.

I noticed that the major roads radiate out from the city's Downtown. Those roads follow what used to be old Indian trails. The Indians would come here from Grand Rapids, Saginaw and Port Huron. All the roads meet at a place called Campus Martius, named after some white guy. Probably Lord Martius or some goofy shit. Drive directly north from Campus Martius for six, seven, eight miles and you'd find those roads.

One of the spokes of the wheel that shoots from Campus Martius is called Gratiot Avenue. I spent my early childhood just south of Gratiot, in a neighborhood once known as Black Bottom. When I drive through there now, I can hardly recognize it. The candy stores, laundromats, pharmacies, drug stores, restaurants and night clubs were all long gone. We would run past a Negro owned funeral home called Lovejoy. Negro owned

Great Lakes Insurance was demolished. As time goes on, I began to forget where some of them were. It's hard to have a frame of reference with a huge fucking freeway sitting where it used to be.

We used to never have to leave the Negro section for anything. Now, I don't want to make it seem like it was perfect. The area was nearly a slum. Homes were nearly older than the city itself. Negroes had been forced to live packed together until white folks began to move to the opens suburbs. But there was so much pride back then, even in our desolation. The city sure has changed. I looked over at Symanski. I guess he had been talking to me.

"Every time I drive up Gratiot, a tear comes to my eyes," he said.

Oh Lord, here we go again.

"Why?" I half-heartedly asked.

"The memories. My aunt Rachel lived up in Roseville. We used to take Gratiot all the way up to see her. Hell, sometimes on Sunday drives when dad was feeling up to it, we'd go all the way out to Port Huron."

I didn't care about his family life. They were probably just as bad as him. But I couldn't pass up the chance to learn some history.

"So, you remember what a lot of this used to look like?"

"Do I? You see right here, up on the right. This used to be Wurm's Recreation Center. We would bowl here all the time. It really is a shame what this city has turned into."

"For once, I agree with you."

"Hard not to, you know? There were businesses all up and down this street. Whatever you wanted, you could have. Hardware stores, movie theatres, candy shops, laundromats, the whole nine. Then Mayor Young came along and fucked it all up. Seventy years of progress and good old fashioned American work ethic, done away in the span of two years."

"But aren't you Polish?"

"Genetically, yes. Culturally, I'm a red blooded American you know?"

"If you're such an American you should know better to save that shit for your little red neck friends, it ain't the mayor's fault."

Mayor Young was my man. One of the few Negro politicians who would tell white folks to kiss his ass. He spoke the truth they didn't want to hear. No one slandered him when I was around.

"Then whose is it?"

"What's Detroit's nickname? The Motor City. You got an entire city that made it big off one thing and one thing only, cars."

"What's your point?" he asked condescendingly.

"What the hell do you think happens when people stop buying cars? Or they move factories to other places?"

"The auto industry don't have nothing to do with all the crime and the fucking riot that made people want to move away. You weren't a cop then, I remember what it was like."

"Negroes ain't no different than any of you. We want to work and live in decent areas. You locked us out of both. What did you think was going to happen?"

"Two wrongs don't make a right you know?"

"What about the first wrong? The police would come into the neighborhoods and beat the shit out of Negroes. We always focus on the response but never what caused it. Besides, what did Dr. King say, riots are the language of the unheard?"

"No, we hear you," he said.

"You just don't care until some shit gets burned up."

"How do you, as a uniformed officer, who is supposed to protect the city, justify burning it down?"

"I don't. But I also understand how the people feel. I was a Negro before I became an officer. I lived in them same areas."

"Well if you don't agree then there shouldn't be nothing more to say about it. Regardless of when white people started leaving the city, burning it down isn't going to make us come back."

"Maybe we don't want y'all back. And the way you're dismissing it right now, is why people burn shit down. It's your job, as an officer to enforce the laws for the community, not just on them. White folks were moving out of the city way before the riots, go sell that shit to someone who don't know."

"If you want to be heard, crime and burning shit isn't the way, you know?"

"I agree."

He turned nice and red.

"Then, well, what else is there to say? If crime ain't the way, that should be it. This city never had crime before, you know?"

"So the Purple Gang never existed? Hell, the FBI was created cause white folks were running wild cutting up so bad. This shit was so lawless they had to create and still operate a whole organization outside of the police to look at the crime."

He didn't talk to me the rest of the ride. Maybe it was something I said. But what could he say? I'm a stone cold killer with facts.

We passed over the interstate. I told him to get into the right lane and begin to slow down. We came to see Johnnie C. Parlor. My time with him wasn't over. I had a lot say. The park was always inhabited by kids whose teachers or parents gave up on them long ago. He was their rings leader.

Smoke whizzed from Symanski's ears. He still fumed over what I told him. He yanked the wheel and made a right on Connor St. I scanned the playground to our right. Did these kids always all dress alike? Were we like that as kids? I doubt it. I searched for a huge Afro and saw thirty of them.

Johnnie liked to be different. He'd wear all black with white shoes. Those gave him away. I told Symanski to park and we hopped out of our cars.

We strolled towards the basketball court. It was nearly surrounded on three sides by red, orange and yellow trees. We had them trapped. By the time they turned and noticed us, I was close enough to chase any one of them down. A fat teen dropped the basketball. He looked as though he was ready to run.

"Don't even think about it," Symanski said. "That just gives me a reason to actually arrest you. Besides, you ain't getting far tubby."

"Fuck you," the fat one said. I spoke to Johnnie.

"Come on, bring your ass. We just need to talk to you. Even if I take you in for being truant, you won't go tomorrow so don't worry. The rest of you can continue. He'll be back in thirty minutes."

Johnnie stepped forward.

"Man, what the fuck y'all want with me? I already told you I didn't see nothing."

"Woah, woah, cool it young blood. I just want to talk you to a place to talk. I need to get inside the mind of a teenager."

He put up a little more of a fuss than I expected but eventually he walked with us to the car. He knew I could make his life hell if he didn't. Symanski drove off. Johnnie stared at his friends outside. Then he turned his hateful gaze to me through the rear view mirror.

There's this unwritten thing that police officers do. I guess white folks in general do it. They see a black child as older than he actually is. They see them as "monsters". "Predators". Vicious "packs of animals". These are just some of the words and phrases I've heard.

I sat around it so much that it would seep into my brain. But I'd always catch that weed and pluck it before I allowed it to plant. I guess the fear began to get to him again because he looked extremely young again to me.

"What do y'all want? If I ain't back in an hour they gone tell my mama. She already knows your name and badge number Dom."

"Be cool young brother. You'll be right back. There's just something we need to show you."

We drove him over to the Jefferson-Chalmers neighborhood. You'd be surprised how many people stick to their section of the city and that's it. They wouldn't know anything about the canals that ran right behind houses over there. A lot of the houses even had boat docks. I hadn't been to too many big cities in America, but I truly thought this was rare.

I had Symanski take us to a park that over looked the Detroit River. A couple fishermen braved the waterfront chill and watched us pull into the parking space. I looked up in the mirror at Johnnie.

"Go on, get out."

We chaperoned him to the railing at the edge of the water. Beyond it, the choppy water rushed pass us. The current looked extra strong that day for some reason. Johnnie through his hands in his pocket. He looked around at the fishermen and turned his head back to us. I guess seeing other people around made him feel bold.

"What? Y'all gonna throw me in? Y'all ain't got the balls."

Symanski looked at me.

"Dom, I don't think he knows just who you are."

"Be cool Symanski, look young brother. Sometimes it's just nice for us to get out of the concrete jungle. Being around all that constant noise really can fuck with you mentally. You get all them outside opinions in your mind and it influences you. You dig what I'm saying?"

"You ain't saying nothing. Take me home."

"We gotta go clear our minds. In the city, we're surrounded by noise and jabber and opinions. You need to come out here more often and free your mind by the water. I used to bring a little fox named Tonia out by the water. We'd smoke a little joint and just float. You gotta try it young blood."

Symanski lit a cigarette and offered one to Johnnie. I leaned against the railing and looked out. There was another small island that I had never been to in front of me. I looked at Symanski.

"What's that little island right there?"

"It's called Peche Island City Park, over on the Canadian side. We get Belle Isle and they get that bull shit."

Maybe pop could bring the boat out next spring. I turned back to the kid.

"Johnnie, as much as you think I'm the enemy, I wanna help."

"Oh, do you?"

"Of course. Just what's your problem with the police?"

"You're a bunch of pigs."

"I've heard, but what's your problem with us. How can I help build trust?"

"Is this a set up?" he asked while he pulled his hands out his pockets. He balled his fists up.

"No man. I told you, be cool."

"Well, for starters y'all can stop beating Negroes down in the streets for the littlest things."

"Okay, what little things? You see my partner is a card carrying Klan member."

Symanski turned his head.

"Ah, blow me Broddie."

I turned back to Johnnie.

"Men like him don't understand what it's like being a Negro nor do they care. So, when you say 'little things', it means nothing to them. What little things exactly do you mean?"

"Okay, like what y'all did to them Panther brothers a couple years ago."

"The ones who did an armed standoff?"

"They was only selling newspapers on the street. What kind of Tom are you?"

Uncle Tom. I had heard that a few times. It's used to describe a Negro who betrays his race and does the bidding for white folks. It comes from the book Uncle Tom's Cabin. Actually Uncle Tom was the hero of the book. Sambo was the term Johnnie should have used.

"I'm not a Tom, trust me."

"Well you sure look like one, you even sound like one."

"I sound like one?" I laughed. "What else Johnnie?"

"Y'all could give Negroes a fair trial."

"Okay done. What else?"

"And, and y'all could quit pulling us over for no reason. Y'all don't do that to them white boys."

"I agree, anything else?"

"It's a lot. I, I just can't think of it now."

I had him. I agreed with many of his points. But I was doing detective work at the time. He could have gone on for three hours about what we did wrong. As soon as he ceased to be able to answer one question, I was going to pounce.

"As I thought. Young brother your heart is in the right place but your mind ain't matching it. You're just repeating shit you don't fully understand. So the next time you try to pull some shit on a cop, make sure it's the right one."

"Fuck off Dom, you're all the same. A bunch of corrupt, no good, trigger happy pigs."

I turned and looked at him. Maybe he did know what he was saying.

"Alright. I tried the human way. Aye Symanski?"

"What?"

"How deep you say that river is?"

"Forty, maybe fifty feet."

"You a good swimmer Johnnie?"

"You wouldn't."

"The next time I see you, I want information you hear me. I want names, dates, pictures and even a mother fucking birth certificate, you dig? Or we just might see how much of a swimmer you really are. Get in the car."

The kid was poised, I'll give him that. He held it together well but it worked. Not only did his eyes soften, but they dropped to the ground. It was quick and he caught it, but I knew I had him.

I would never actually throw a fucking kid in the river, or even the canal. But I had known that kid since he was twelve when I patrolled his apartment building. He was a little shit and that was the best way to get through to him.

I graduated from the school of doing what needed to be done. If by scaring him, I would be solving a case and saving more lives, then so be it. He wasn't an innocent bystander, he knew something and sometimes you have to bend the rules. Hell, I learned from the best.

7

Chapter 7

I did mention that community outreach was the hardest part of this job right? We looked like Jehovah's Witnesses when we got back to the crime scene neighborhood. Door after door was shut in our faces, if they were opened at all. Granted, it was a Wednesday morning. Many people were probably at work. But if unemployment was as high as the news said it was, more people should have been able to open their doors.

Our job was fully of irony. They got tough on crime to stop crime. But by treating everyone the same, we ended up creating the same animosity and criminality that we were looking to erase. We did the same shit in Vietnam.

They thought that burning shit up was putting a dent in recruitment. All the VC had to do was come to a burned down village after Americans came through. We turned it into a hotbed for recruitment.

Our higher ups couldn't understand why if you kill one VC, ten more replaced him. On the streets of Detroit, you mistreat one brother, ten more felt his pain and took up arms against you. I think they'd get paid enough to recognize that shit. Maybe they designed it to be this way.

We tried not to speak above a whisper. The other neighbors would hear everything that was said in the quiet, working class neighborhood. After thirty minutes of being rejected and ignored, we finally hit a winner.

When the door opened, a pair of mysterious brown eyes stared at me. It was the woman who had walked away from me earlier. She might have been perhaps a few years older than me. Her body and looks remained intact. But I could tell, after a few more years of whatever she was doing, they would hit rock bottom. She yawned and stretched her arms at the door.

"You again?" she said from behind the screen door. "It's really impolite to follow a lady."

She wasn't a lady. A lady doesn't open the door in a robe. Sometimes it was worth it to flirt with the women. I've always been able to charm my way into some information.

"I keep running into you. It's a sign," I said.

"It's a sign that I need to move. Y'all get in here before somebody sees you."

A log was smoldering in the fireplace at the far side of the room. She told us to have a seat at the dining room table. I couldn't help but notice the switch in her walk as she went into the hallway. The toys she tossed into the downstairs bedroom made loud clangs against the radiator.

Other than those toys, the house was immaculate. Spotless floors. Well organized photos on the fireplace mantle. A plastic covering protected on the pink and green floral pattern sofa. The vibrant purple on the wall paper strangely soothed me. The most prominent feature was an enormous poster of Jesus. Draped in a purple robe, it looked good on his dark skin. His hair was nappy and beautiful. She caught me staring at it.

"My cousin painted that for me. He said that's what Jesus really looked like."

She walked into the spotless kitchen that didn't have a single dirty dish in it. The linoleum floors looked to be new. Her home needed some repairs, but whose didn't? Compared to the other homes we had entered, this was a palace. She called out to us.

"Y'all want some water, juice?"

"No, thank you," I said.

I answered for Symanski. He'd rather sip on sand than drink out of a Negro's home. She ran up the steps and came back down seconds later with a purple blouse and some blue jeans. Maybe she was a lady. The night gown might have been inappropriate but I wasn't complaining about it.

I was glad she did. I didn't want Symanski to see her like that. Them racist bastards love trying to get some from a Negro woman. I heard one say "You ain't a man until you done it with a Negro." That shit makes my skin crawl. She leaned over and opened the window next to the table. She sat at the table with us.

Whatever attraction I felt for her went away with the flick of a lighter. She puffed on that cigarette and blew the smoke out the window. I can't stand a woman that smokes. Hate it. It's like kissing an ashtray. I want a woman, not a God damn construction worker. She stared at me.

"You want one?"

"No, I'm good."

"What about your buddy?"

Symanski reached his hand out to the pack that sat on the ripped up table. I grabbed his hand and stopped him. I still can't make sense of why. I guess it's like I said, I don't like white boys looking at sisters that way. Him grabbing a cigarette from her would connect them in some way. It's strange but it made sense in the moment.

"What's your name again Detective?" she asked.

She crossed her legs. Damn she was sexy without even trying. Her voice was velvet smooth. Man was I scared of her.

I gave her both of our names.

"Pleasure to meet you gentlemen. My name is Vaughn Turner."

"I hope we didn't catch you at a bad time?"

"Of course you did but I'm up now."

"I'd hate for your husband to walk in and see you sitting with two men at his table."

"Well Detective you don't have to worry about that for two reasons. One, this is my table and two, if my husband shows up here then we have deeper problems than a murder."

"Why's that?" Symanski asked.

"He's been dead damn near six years now. See that picture up on my mantle behind you? That's my Nolan."

In the photo, they leaned up against a car while he held her in his arms. Damn, she was drop dead gorgeous.

"What happened to him, if you don't mind me asking?"

"Nolan, heh," she scoffed, "he survived them jungles of Vietnam and came home just to be killed gambling by some dope fiend. It was in the papers. Actually..."

She stood up and wiggled into the living room. Her face was buried in folders with photos and newspaper clippings. She came back to the table and tossed a cut out on the table.

"Local War Hero Slain Over Twenty Dollars" it read.

"From what he told me, over there, they used to have to smoke the dope instead of snorting it cause it was so strong. So when he got back, his habit was so bad that he needed more of the weak shit here to feel normal again. He was so fucking stupid."

He looked familiar. I had known many men like Nolan. It was common really. I don't think they knew just what them drugs would do to them. That's what kept me away from them. Yeah, I was called a square, but one thing nobody ever gone call me is somebody's junkie. Them sunken eyes. Scratching like nobody's watching. Open sores all over the body. Looking and acting like a fucking zombie. No way Jack, not me.

"How long was he over there?" I asked.

"He only went once for like a year. I think in seventy. He left a strong black brother and came back a junkie. He had a lot of good shit going before that. A good gig down at the plant that bought us this house."

"How have you been getting by since?"

"I work down at Michigan Bell. It ain't much but I'm blessed to have it. But y'all didn't come to hear my problems."

Symanski stepped in.

"Right, so what do you know about what happened at the corner up there?"

"I sent my oldest two off to school when I saw what was happening at the corner over there. Hell, you probably know more than me. Some pigs got blasted."

"You didn't happen to see anything did you?"

She took another puff.

"Nope but things been real hot over this way lately."

"What do you mean?"

"A whole bunch of these young boys been acting wild as of recent."

"Any in particular?"

She tapped the ash in the ash tray and thought for a moment.

"How much time you got? But if I had to pick the wildest that I've seen, it's this little high yellow nigga that's down the street all the time. I think his daddy was French or something like that."

"A mulatto?"

"Yeah, he look like it. He got the hair like one."

This could have been one of our shooters.

"What's his name?"

"I don't know that but he look like he about sixteen, seventeen. The boy is always loud. Him and his little pals hang at this house down the street. It's on the opposite side of the street. You can't miss the red awning on it, only one on the block with it."

"When's the last time you saw him?"

"Last weekend probably. If it was anyone you're looking for that did something around here, it'd be him."

We both stood up.

"Where are y'all going?"

"We're going to go see if he's there," I said.

"Right after leaving my house down the street? This why don't nobody talk to y'all. What are you rookies? At least drive around for a few minutes, Jesus Christ."

"Sorry about that Mrs. Turner. We-"

"It's Ms. Turner. Remember, my husband went and got himself killed."

"Sorry Ms. Turner, we'll drive around for a minute but I do have one more question for you."

"Shoot."

"Why? Why speak to us?"

"Well earlier I didn't want nobody to see me talking to you. It's bad for business. Y'all ain't exactly angels you know. But

I'm speaking now because I'm just tired. I'm tired of it all you know? All the little bullshit, excuse my language Lord. I guess it wouldn't bother me so much if it wasn't some innocent folks getting hurt. That bothers me Detective Broddie."

"Thank you, Ms. Turner. Here are our cards, don't hesitate to call us with anything you need."

"Remember you said that Detective."

We stepped outside and got into Symanski's car.

"Boy did she want to fuck you," Symanski said. "Go do it, it shouldn't take long. You pump her for the best three minutes of her life and we get back to work."

"Pull off God damn it."

"Really? I didn't take you for a fairy. Suit yourself."

He grinned and pulled off.

We didn't go far. The area was lined with businesses. Auto shops, electronic repair stores, toy stores, you name it. The owners gave us an ear full. All we got from them was that we don't show up enough in the area. They pay their taxes just like the rest and blah blah. Ironically, when the police did show up in the neighborhood, they got shot at.

Those four visits didn't really amount to much, nor did we expect them to. We had the house we wanted and it was time to go see our little mulatto friend.

We parked right in front of the small home. These thin little bed sheets covered the window. The bushes grew wild to the right of the porch. We got out and walked up to it. I could feel the eyes on my back. Everyone in the neighborhood seemed to be watching. Even the people who refused to open the doors.

Symanski banged on the door. We waited for a while with no answer. He banged again. Next door, the front door creaked open.

"It's abandoned," said the elderly man.

"Do you ever see anyone in here?"

"No sir."

He closed the door and that was the last we saw of him. If anyone was inside, they weren't coming out, and we couldn't go in. Well not legally at least.

"Wanna write up a warrant?" I asked Symanski.

"Let's do it."

8

Chapter 8

I could hear the clicking noises from our department while we were still outside the precinct. They'd drive you crazy if you let them. Typing had never really been my strong suit. I either felt like a sissy secretary or some caveman sitting there hunched over at the desk. I never knew where to place my hands. I just pressed the keys one by one. If I was bad, Symanski was worse. Tap, tap, growl, slap. He thrust his chair back from the desk. He threw his hands behind his neck as he turned towards me.

"You finished yet?"

"Get off my ass, I'm working on it."

"If I wanted someone to drag ass on this thing, I would've partnered up with Walters. Oh hey Walters, didn't see you there."

The detectives sat along a long aisle that we called the "Avenue of Investigation", with Mitchell's office at the end of it. Detective Adam Walters waddled through it to Symanski's desk. He looked like a parade float coming down the aisle. The aged wood creaked as he plopped his formless body on the desk. He turned his head over to me and raised his #1 Dad coffee mug and took a long sip. Of all the white folks in the office, Walters might have been the one I disliked the least. He was somewhat decent. He never really said anything bad to me. But then again, he never really said anything at all.

He would just nod his head or raise his cup. You just know when you make someone uncomfortable. That's how I felt with Walters. I didn't mind it though. If you have a problem with me, you don't have to deal with me. Chances are I wouldn't like you anyway.

"Georgie, Georgie, Georgie," Walters said. "What have you gotten yourself into now?"

"I hit the jackpot this time Walters," Symanski said.

"Either that or Mitchells doesn't like Pollocks."

"It might be both."

"Whichever it is, you sir, are looking at a rough, unsolvable case."

"How do you figure that fat boy?"

"You think they are going to talk? They hate cops. They probably think that getting rid of two was doing them a favor."

I did my best to focus on my typing. Walters continued.

"No one is gonna give them up. They're probably on a couch in someone's basement with their feet kicked up like nothing ever happened."

"You're out of touch with the community fatso. My soul brother Dom used a little bit of that inner Billy Dee Williams. Not only did he get a woman to talk, but we got a description of a potential suspect."

"Did he now?"

"Yessir. We're on our way to search the kid's house right now. I'll make a Detective out of Broddie yet."

"So you're soul brothers now?" Walters asked me. "I didn't

63

know you two were sweet on each other."

I looked over at him in disbelief. I had gotten used to him not talking to me so I didn't know what to say. My throat tightened a bit. I felt uncomfortable.

"Fuck no," I said as I turned my head back to the typewriter.

Wendell told me the keys to surviving on this job. Keep your head low and mind your own business. I wouldn't keep my head low, but my business was just that.

"Broddie, you could fuck almost every broad in the city, but that ain't going to get them to trust us."

"Well don't stop the boy from trying," Symanski smiled. "You're just mad that your four-inch cock couldn't do the trick."

They laughed. That was actually funny but I'd chuckle later.

"Georgie, just last year alone there were over two thousand complaints against the police. To them, a cop being dead means one less complaint to file."

"But this one was a Negro. They'll talk."

"I don't know, sounds like a 'chicken coming home to roost' type thing."

"You know what they need to do?"

"What's that Georgie?"

"They need to train them God damn cops the right way and this wouldn't happen."

Walters must've known what Symanski meant before I did. He looked at him and said "Hey Georgie, why don't you cool it?"

But once Symanski got going, there was no stopping him. As I said before, he meant what he said. If it came out his mouth, you best believe it was how he felt. He was not shy about letting the world know.

"They aren't training them properly is all I'm saying. They just say, hey brother, you're a Negro. There's a lot of Negroes in the city, come on it and work for us. Can you shoot a gun? Chase a suspect? Control a hostile situation? No? Shit, come in and be a cop anyway."

Walters was uncomfortable. He was trying to look for ways out of the conversation. Symanski interrupted him at every turn.

"Nowadays, any fucking schmuck can wear a badge and carry a gun. We got good-hard working men who are being passed over these jobs just to give it to some Negro. Then they go and replace the chief with-"

"God damn it Georgie. That's enough," Walters cut in.

"No, you stop me when I'm saying something wrong. Now, it ain't about them being Negroes. Some of my closet friends are Negroes. I just want a cop who can do a decent fucking job. Wendell, you're a sensible guy, back me up here."

Wendell had this almost comical nonchalance about him.

"Fuck off, Symanski," he said. Walters stepped in again.

"I don't know, Symanski. A lot of other cops got the job just because they were white, so how do you explain that? I mean look at Gentry over there. He can't read or write and he's a lead detective."

Walters smiled at the balding man who looked up from his desk. I didn't see him but knowing him, he probably gave Walters a healthy middle finger. Symanski kept on talking.

"Look, they need to be taught to do the job properly. Maybe then shit like what happened this morning wouldn't be so common."

I tried my best to ignore it, I really did but somebody had to call this shit out.

"Are you saying it's Lyles' fault that he was shot?"

"Did I say that? It ain't his fault he got shot. But it is his fault for not following the right procedure in a hostile environment."

Just like that, it was on. It never took much to get Symanski and I going. He preached about the unwritten book of police procedures. And how Lyles was trying to show Cooke some "Negro solidarity" and how much control he had over the situation. I couldn't believe it. Here he was blaming the man for his own death.

He brought up the "Big Four" and "S.T.R.E.S.S" departments. Two units that were notorious for brutalizing Negro men. Just three years prior, a former officer was dismissed from the force after haven taken part in nine killings and three nonfatal shootings. Ironically, units such as those were the very thing that made riots, or rebellions even possible.

Our back and forths were very commonplace. Often, some of the other detectives would sit back in their seats and grab some popcorn. The week before, Walters walked over and stirred the pot. He simply said that Ken Norton beat Muhammad Ali in their fight in September. He knew I was an Ali fan and it didn't take much to get me going.

It wasn't so much that Symanski liked Norton, he just hated a loud, brazen black man who told off white folks. I wasn't too fond of the draft dodging, but I could overlook it.

As he and I continued our battle, Walters took a step back and apologized for even walking over. It was too late. The motor was already running. Usually I would threaten to kick Symanski's ass six times before we had our morning coffee. Of course he didn't want any of that. Punk motherfucker.

He's got a lot to say until it's time to back it up. I tried to keep my cool. I wouldn't want Chelle to see me like that. From the stories I've told her, I'm sure she thinks I'm some violent man without a soul. But that day, she was close to seeing who I really was. Symanski and I stood up when another cigarette damaged voice shot through the room.

"I thought I told you two sissies to cut this shit out," it yelled. Mitchells stomped down the aisle and stopped within ten feet of us. Any closer and he probably would've been caught in the crossfire. He continued.

"Actually, how's this? You two can stay right here and bash each other's brains out. Is that what you want, Symanski?"

"No sir but I-"

"But shit. While you're fighting, I'll call your wives and tell them to go find new men to fuck cause you'll both be out of a job. As a matter of fact, both of you, in my office right now."

God how I hated taking orders from anyone. Even as a child. My pop would always have me call him sir and stand at attention and shit. Looking back, I think even he sees what kind of crap that was.

It's kind of funny that I went to the military because I naturally went against orders. Who the hell are you to tell me what to do? That's why I did my years and got out.

My natural response to an order was "Or what?" "What the hell are you going to do if I don't?" So imagine the embarrassment I felt as I walked down the aisle. Everyone in there knew that about me. I wondered if they took pride in seeing me broken. Wendell flashed me a look of pity.

I would have rather done that talk in a Cambodian bathhouse than in Mitchells' office. Any room he walked in immediately became small and cramped. What's worse, he was the biggest Jets fan I had ever seen. Every inch of his wall was covered with green and white. He loved Joe Namath more than Jesus.

The worst part about it was a picture he had of Rocky Marciano. What a fucking joke. He wasn't no real champion and damn sure couldn't bang with them boys today. Jimmy Young, Norton, Ali. They would eat that white boy up.

Mitchells went straight behind his desk. He stood strong and upright, courtesy of his military background. Thank God his huge frame blocked that horrible ass picture.

Symanski shut the door behind him. We both remained standing. Carefully studied by Mitchells' grey eyes. His stare was very familiar to me. He scanned for any sign of weakness. A twitch. A fidget. A gulp, anything to show you weren't comfortable. When they found it, they'd pounce.

"What the hell is going on with you two maggots?"

I wasn't about to let Symanski control the conversation. It wasn't in me.

"Nothing we couldn't settle."

"It didn't sound like nothing."

We remained silent. I began to shake. This took me back to my school days. I never started trouble. But I damn sure finished it. I was a grown ass man. Don't lecture me like a child. Mitchells continued.

"I'm sick and tired of opening that door and hearing you two fairies argue about everything but some God damn cases. Whether it be Elvis, Motown or slavery, I'm tired of hearing it."

Symanski had a smug grin on his face. I guess he figured his brethren would take his side.

"Now I hear you trashing the God damn Chief Symanski. I got one dead cop and another with bullets in his chest and an angry public that's demanding answers that you two haven't given me."

There was power in his voice. His gray skin began to flash

68

red.

"Not only are you two still in this God damn office but you're sitting here going at each other's throats like a couple of third grade lovers. Now, I'll ask you once more, what the hell is going on here?"

I'm glad he stopped when he did. He wasn't winning any marathons in his shape. Any longer without taking a breath and Symanski would've had to perform mouth to mouth. I spoke up.

"Like we said, nothing. It's normal."

"Final answer?"

We both nodded our heads.

"Do you know that there's a betting pool on who wins the fight between you two?"

"Who'd you pick?" I asked him.

Symanski smirked but Mitchells didn't find it funny. He leaned back on the window sill. I could see Marciano's glove.

"It seems my little experiment with you two has failed then."

Experiment? Like I'm some animal. I knew it. Mitchells hated to see a young brother that was going to pass him up one day.

"Symanski, you're a bigot. And I'd know, I used to be one, but-"

I stopped myself from shaking my head. There was always a "but" whenever I agreed with a white person. He continued.

"Broddie, you're too arrogant to learn anything. The two of you are done together. Symanski you stay on the Lyles case and Broddie, I have something special for you. Fresh off the presses."

Those words hurt. I was meant to be on that murder case. If I could solve that, I'd be Chief within ten years. Mitchells was hip to that and was throwing me off the fast track, that son of a bitch.

"Sir, how is that fair? We were making good progress on that case."

"By sitting in the office yelling at each other?"

"But-"

"Broddie that's an order."

Somehow Mitchells survived the D-Day invasion. He always used military lingo when talking to me. He knew I hated that word "order".

"You two will kill each other before you even find the fucking killers."

I decided to let Symanski talk.

"Sir we actually don't work bad together. We just have normal differences."

"Ahh bullshit Symanski. Go feed that sweet lipped bullshit to your wife cause I ain't buying it. You two need the time apart anyway."

I waited for him to call Wendell in the room. I had always wanted to work with the brother. We'd be a dynamite match. His calm coolness and my aggressive go get 'em attitude? We'd be a number one spot on CBS prime time.

"That's all Symanski. Get back to work," Mitchells said.

Symanski stood up and patted my shoulders as he walked out. I watched Mitchells, looking for signs of weakness.

"This is bullshit Lieutenant," I said. I came off more aggressive than I meant to. But the rage built up in me. It had to come out.

"Take it easy, Broddie. It's my job to place my detectives where we will succeed as a department. It ain't about individual accolades and who solves what."

"I was in a position to win. Symanski doesn't know or care shit about the community. That case would have-"

I had said too much.

"Would have what?" he folded his arms. "I'll remind you, these cases are not for you to make a name off of."

"Yes sir."

"These are people's lives you are dealing with."

"Yes sir."

"You determine how families sleep at night."

"Yes sir. I just take that one personal is all."

"We all do. But with the way things are going, there will be more unfortunately."

He sighed and sat in the chair. Marciano stared at me again.

"Now, onto the case I have for you. You're familiar with our old friend Reverend Wallace Brown?"

"How could I forget him? He was out there this morning half ass preaching."

"Yes will that area is very hot today."

"What are you asking me to do for him?"

"He needs help Dom."

"Sir, but isn't that in the seventh precinct?"

"They're swamped right now and need help. All of that shit with him is in the past. He's actually done some good for the community."

I rubbed my face with my palms. I didn't notice but my hands had begun to sweat.

"What's the case?"

"He can't find his son. Thinks the boy may be missing."

"Sir, a missing kid who probably isn't even missing?"

"It might not sound like much but it's just as fulfilling. If the boy isn't missing then it gives you and Symanski some time to

71

cool down."

"But sir-"

"Look God damn it. That's the case. Now don't make a jack ass out of me. That case is yours or you can go work for Chrysler."

"Yes sir."

I stood up. I had half a mind to toss my badge at him. Did I mention I hate being told what to do? Missing persons cases were the absolute worst. Nine times out of ten the person ran away and came back with or without you. Homicides were more fun. They had a lot more action. As I walked out the door, he called me.

"He probably isn't missing Dom. This doesn't happen in Detroit. Maybe in Oakland County but not here. Just go check up on it."

I didn't respond.

9

Chapter 9

The Reverend's storefront church fit him perfectly. Small and cramped, with a funky odor. I'm sure he was refused access to preach inside a real church. The insurance companies probably didn't want to cover a building that would for sure be struck by lightning. It was very easy to miss the building. It looked just like the hundreds of other storefronts that sat on Van Dyke Avenue. A pathetic banner flapped in the wind. It read "Gethsemane Tabernacle Ministries".

I had half a mind to leave right then and there. I was sure all this madness would settle itself. What was Mitchells thinking? He always gives the Negroes the short end of the stick. If I didn't have two mouths to feed, I would've walked right up to him and told him just where he can go. But no one wants to be the man who tells his wife that they have to go hungry that night.

When I passed the side street a group of teenagers all turned their heads at me. They stood at the bottom of a porch. They had to be at least sixteen years old. I studied them. Running the descriptions we had been given through my mind. None of them looked to be mulatto.

The church door swung open. Slimy and full of himself, the Reverend slithered out, carrying a box of food. A woman followed him to her car. Her hands made a praying gesture in front of her face. She thanked him and hopped in the late model Chevy and was quick to pull off. The Reverend's feet might have been too heavy to pick up. He slid them across the concrete. He didn't see me until he came near the door.

He was an old cat for sure. But other than his balding head, he didn't look his age. Negroes are usually like that. I got an uncle Freddie that's in his late fifties but doesn't look a day over forty.

The Reverend didn't seem to recognize me. How could he have forgotten? Did he not remember me from earlier? Did he not remember me from a few years ago? I walked towards him to speak. My mama and daddy raised me right. Even with our ongoing beef, I was still respectful.

"Hey, uh, you're Reverend Brown?"

"Yes, yes I am son. Who might you be?"

I introduced myself. His eyes sparkled. I stuck my hand out to meet his. Shouldn't no grown man walk around with a soft hand shake like that. It says a lot about him. And it told me that everything I had already suspected was true. Soft, timid, weak. Easy to sway. Prone to fits of emotional outbursts.

What was even worse was the terrible smell. From ten feet away, even in the outside air, the stench attacked me. I'm a beer man myself. Never was into heavy alcohol, but I know whiskey when I smell it. It wasn't even good whiskey. My stomach began a spin cycle as I got closer to him.

He invited me inside the building. His lair looked better than I expected, but that ain't saying much. Even with the lights on, the building was still dark and dull. Easter Sundays in this den couldn't have been filled with much inspiration. I think good ole Jesus would skip this "tabernacle" on his reunion tour.

The foyer made a sharp turn into the main room. A couple dozen chairs formed long rows of makeshift pews. At the altar were two uniformed officers that I recognized. Two white boys that in all actuality, I never had any problems with. They were respectful to me and I to them. They spoke to a tall Negro when Brown interrupted.

He introduced them all to me. The tall Negro was his youngest brother. He was a Deacon at the church named Jeremiah Brown They might have been distant cousins with how opposite they were. Even down to their handshakes. Then he directed my attention to a dark corner of the room.

Some crazy looking thing rocked back and forth in a chair. Its hair sat wild and untouched, covering its face. Only the Exorcist made more of an impression on me. I balled my fist up as it clutched onto a Bible and whispered to itself.

It was his wife, Pam. She roosted in that corner and spat out more "Our Fathers" than I had said my whole life. The Reverend tiptoed over to her. His hands were out in front of him as if he approached an animal.

I turned and spoke to the Deacon who at least had a spirit of truth. He told me about his father's "exaggerations". He had heard them his whole life. He always had an agenda but doubted that he would do so with his own child. But I knew that anything was possible with this man.

After the two officers told me absolutely nothing, I called the Reverend back over. I played it cool.

"I need a statement from you Reverend. Tell me everything you can about him."

"He's uh…" He took a sip of water. "Well his name is mine. Wallace Brown. But everybody just calls him Junior. He's eleven-years-old. A skinny kid with a big old head."

The Reverend continued to describe his son. Perhaps missing a child took its toll on him, but he rambled as if he had never really seen the boy. I jotted down anything I deemed to be truth.

"We have good kids. No enemies," he said.

"What about you?"

"Oh heavens no. I'm one of the most beloved figures in this neighborhood."

I'm sure.

"So there's no trouble you've ever been in?"

"Not since I left Sweet Home, Arkansas."

"And when was that?"

"I think I was about Junior's age. It was so long ago."

"You looked to be in your fifties?" I asked him.

"Yes. In my fifties."

"How long have you and your wife been married?"

"Detective stop me if I'm being rude but why?"

"I need to get a full understanding of the situation."

"Are you looking for me or him?"

His eyes showed slight irritation. I decided to pull back.

"Sir, these questions all help point me towards the boy."

"Right. Well we've been married for twenty years now."

"So she isn't Jeremiah's mother?" I pointed to his wife. He cut his eyes at me.

"What makes you say that Detective?"

"Jeremiah just looks like he's older than twenty is all. I mean nothing by it."

I didn't mean anything by it. At least not intentionally.

"No," he said. "She isn't his mother biologically, but she is in spirit. We are all one big spiritual family."

"I see. And when did you last see Junior?"

He gave me a long drawn out story. Junior returned home from school and went to the store up the street. He forgot something and went back out to get it. An hour later his mother realized he didn't come back home. They went around the neighborhood looking for him and no one saw a thing.

He gave me the minute details of his son's usual day. What time he wakes up. The school he goes to. His teacher's names. When I asked if the boy would have any reason to run away, he looked offended.

"Run away?" he said. "From one of the most respected families on the east side of the city? No, no, no, no. If anything, his friends should be running away to here."

I asked who he had in the church that day. From volunteering to mentoring, the Reverend led a busy week. He gave me a rundown of the names. No one stood out and besides, they all left by the time Junior disappeared. With no lead, I asked to see the boy's room.

He led me into the back room. A door on the left wall opened up to some steps. I followed him up the steep stairs. I wondered what he had heard about Lyle's murder. I needed to think about something to distract myself from that stench seeping from his pores.

We emerged from the cold, damp and dark downstairs. A lovely pink color and the smell of lilac greeted us. The upstairs looked to be in a completely different building. He even made me take my shoes off before I entered.

Two adorable little girls laid on the couch together. Their eyes remained fixed on Scooby Doo. The oldest couldn't have been any older than Tasha. He introduced them to me. They shyly waved and then were sent into their room.

Brown led me into the hallway. He stopped at the last door and turned the ceramic knob.

"Just like he left it," Brown said.

The bed sat tight against the wall. It was made with military precision. Better than any bed I had ever made. The action figures were arranged by height on the dresser. His shoes lined against the back wall.

I asked if Brown had noticed anything missing. He hadn't. I went to the dresser and moved one of the cars. I left the back wheel out of line with the car next to it. I could tell this bothered the Reverend. I walked over to the bed and knelt down. Under the bed was spotless as well.

"It's strange that a kid keeps his room this clean," I said.

"No, no. Cleanliness is next to Godliness Detective. My wife keeps a very neat household. Proverbs chapter twelve verse-"

I went deaf at that point. I wasn't there for a sermon. The boy's book case had a copy of Treasure Island. Its condition showed that he read it more than the Bible next to it. I thumbed through it.

"He's an adventurous boy huh?"

"He loves Pirates, cowboys and Indians. We tried to get him out of it but he refuses."

I put the book back. I searched through everything. Closets, under beds and cupboards. All the usual hiding places. Nothing out of the ordinary caught my eye until I went back into the living room. A photo of Reverend Brown and the mayor. They had their arms around each other. They smiled into the camera like old friends.

"How well do you know him?" I asked.

"He's supported some of my programs. I helped get him

elected. He's a good buddy of mine. I can call him up at any moment."

I didn't believe it but if it was true, I could use this. I juggled the two cases in my mind. I went back to checking the house. It was too nice. People never stay this clean unless they were hiding something. I turned to him.

"This is your church right Mr. Brown?"

"Yessir. Started it here from nothing."

"And you maintain it by yourself?"

"Well my son and wife help but other than that, yes. It is all me."

"So that doesn't leave you with much time for your children? Being a pillar of the community and such?"

"Well now, no. I spend a whole heap of time with my children."

"But if-"

"But nothing," he said, growing angry. "Now people call me a lot of things, Detective. Some may be true but an unfit father is not one of them."

"Reverend I-"

"Through all I've gone through in my life, and the mistakes I made with my first born, those children are well looked after."

"I'm sorry Reverend. I didn't mean it in that way."

He folded his arms.

"What I'm meaning to say is, has Junior ever done something like this before?"

He hesitated.

"Reverend, I need you to be honest with me. It's the only way we can piece together what happened."

"Well, it's not unusual for him to be gone for hours at a time. We keep a tight leash but he's a kid. He's never been gone this long and it just don't feel right, Detective."

"I see. And has he ever shown forms of rebellion?"

"How do you mean?"

Back from the loony bin, his wife opened the door to the upstairs. She looked better but not by much. Surprisingly, she could speak.

"Wallace, he's asking you if you think Junior ran away from home."

Brown ran over to her and helped her to the couch. He handed her a glass of water. Damn her. I almost had him. Now he would clam up. As strange as she was, I was still raised with manners.

"Not in those terms ma'am. We just deal with this a lot. Maybe he needed to get away from it all?"

If looks could kill, I would've been laid out on the carpet. She slammed the glass down. Water splashed all over her hand.

"My son did not need 'time away from it all'. He is a good boy and is missing. You're wasting precious time sitting here acting like we know something when we don't. You should be out there looking for him."

"Ma'am, you know him the best. Who better to ask? It's my job to ask these questions, even if they are uncomfortable."

"Do you have any children?"

She and I went back and forth for the next ten minutes. I did my best to be polite. I really did. But she kept gnawing away at my competence. I cut her off repeatedly and didn't feel bad for it. All signs did point to her son running away. I shouldn't feel bad for thinking it.

We only stopped when I attempted to sweet talk her. Her uttering the word "bullshit" was too much for the Reverend to handle. She hated me. I could see it in her eyes. I guess I couldn't blame her. She believed her boy was missing. Who was I to tell her different?

Brown led me out of the room. Her gaze burned some of the hair off the back of my head. We continued going down the steps. Her voice still followed me until we hit the bottom of the steps. I began to search around the church in the same way.

Once again I found no sign of the boy. I decided to go to the store where he was last seen. Maybe they would have some answers. As I began to walk out the door, Brown called to me.

"Don't you at least need a picture of him?"

Jesus Christ, how could I forget that? Seeing this man had my mind all over the place.

I confirmed it and sent him up the stairs to retrieve it. Churches usually made me feel stiff. Like if I made any wrong move, I would be persecuted. My body immediately relaxed when I stepped outside. A cool breeze blew some leaves by me. God was it warm and stale in there.

That boy was out here somewhere. I looked at the cemetery across the street. No, too creepy. Wouldn't no child hide there. Behind me the door opened. Brown shoved the photo in my face.

It was a school picture that had been taken in April of that year. He had on the same outfit today. Some blue jeans, a blue sweater and black Converse shoes.

"Ok Reverend," I said. "I'm going to call this in right away and begin to investigate."

"Thank you Detective. We need to find him."

"Yes, however, I do have one question for you."

"Anything."

"Walk with me."

I led him further down Van Dyke. I towered over his balding head. We walked about fifteen seconds when I stopped him.

"Do you know about what happened up there this morning?"

"Yes, I led the people in prayer."

"Right, well we're looking for four Negro teenage suspects. I think the cases may be related."

A little lie never really hurt anyone. I had to do anything to solve these cases. I was supposed to feel shame for intertwining the cases but I didn't. Children typically show up a day or two after they are reported missing. He was fine. The Reverend didn't bite.

"How so?" he asked. "What would that have to do with my son?"

"We just believe they are related. I don't want to say too much right now. Just keep your ears open for anything."

"Okay Detective."

With parting words he informed me of the search that he had organized for the next morning. I almost felt bad for the bastard. His eyes shook and began to gloss. I shook his limp hand and turned to walk away. He called back to me.

"Detective, uh, just, one more thing. Please, well, I, I'm begging you, please take this serious. It's not like him. And, I'm not saying you aren't but I just want to stress this."

"Reverend I'll treat it like he is my son."

I guess his wife forced him to say that to me. She stood at the door of the church. Those piercing eyes followed me again. I don't blame her though. My mother would have lit Camp Pendleton on fire if I didn't return from Vietnam in one piece. It's what a parent was supposed to do.

10

Chapter 10

The store was only a quarter of a mile away. I decided to take in some of the lovely scenery. A fresh Savannah of grass waved in a vacant lot. A huge mural of Jesus. Black, bearded and draped in purple, he held his hands out to the world. I'm not a religious cat but I dug it. I kept my eyes open for anything out of the ordinary.

An old cat stood outside the store. He reclined against the peeling white paint as if he owned the building. His long, grey locks touched his shoulder. He threw out filthy hands when I came towards him. Covered in dirt and grime, I wouldn't touch them with a stick. I ignored him and walked inside. It had been a long day and I was in no mood.

The atmosphere was tense when I pushed open the door. This Chaldean cat stood behind the counter. At least I think he was Chaldean. He had to be sixty years old. His spitting image sat at the opposite end of the counter. They turned their heads from the TV and watched me. Their stores were among Negroes. You'd think they would be comfortable around us by now.

I gave them the same old spiel. My name and title. The badge

I held up relieved their fears a bit. The father breathed again and introduced the duo. His name was Natan and his son was Josep. They both seemed rattled.

"I'm investigating a missing boy named Wallace Brown Jr. He was at your store earlier this afternoon?"

"Oh, yes, yes, little Junior. His father is the Reverend down the street. Good boy, good boy. Why do you ask?"

"His mother said she sent him here earlier to pick up groceries?"

"No, no, I haven't seen Wallace all week."

I glared at him. Why would he lie about that?

"Well, Natan, I happen to know that's not true. He was in this store earlier wasn't he?"

"No, no, no, he uh, didn't come this way."

"Are you sure Nathan? With one call I can have a perimeter set up around this place to search it from top to bottom."

He looked over to his son. They both might have shit their pants. It's a scary thought. To be thought to be in connection with a missing Negro kid. I'm sure they could picture five hundred Negroes outside their door. Foaming at the mouth with pitch forks and torches. He cracked.

"Alright, alright. He was in here earlier. But he came in to get the butter and I hadn't seen him since."

"Then why would you lie about that?"

"His father and I had bad words for each other and I don't want you to think we did it."

"What kind of bad words?"

"Well he's a good kid but he lets his friends control him. I caught them stealing over the summer and I chased them out. His papa wasn't too happy about it."

"What'd he do about it?"

84

"He cursed the boy in a way I never saw before. Told him how wrong it was and God hates a thief."

"Well that's not so bad," I replied. I had been cursed out myself.

"There's more. He then turns to curse at me and call me out my name. He told me to never yell at his boy."

I shook my head. That sounds like the man I knew. He continued.

"We got into a small fight but it finished with happy days. We have been fine since then."

"And that's why you lied?"

"Yes, well, I didn't want you to think I did it. It's his word against mine."

"So, he left right after? Did you see which way he went when he walked out?"

"No, I'm sorry, I didn't pay attention."

I spun around in a circle and took careful inventory of it. He's not here, I thought to myself. I did my due diligence. I turned back to the father.

"Well I have two questions. One can I place flyers in your window tomorrow?"

"Of course."

"Good. The second is about that murder earlier this morning."

"Yes, it has all of us on edge. I have never felt like I needed a gun until now."

"Yes, well, I have reason to believe they are connected. What I need from you is to keep an ear out for me alright?"

I handed him a business card.

"If my partner, a funny looking white cat, visits you soon, just keep this between us."

85

"Uh sure thing Detective. But if you really want to know what's going on around here, ask those no-good kids outside."

He pointed to a pair of white Converse shoes in a sea of black. The group had just walked up to the store. I knew very well who they belonged too. Perfect timing. I needed to speak with him anyway.

I thanked the two of them and shoved the store door open. It made a loud plastic bang when I hit it. The boys jumped and turned towards me. Johnnie Parlor hung his head in disappointment while his friends ran in the opposite direction.

I brought up how ironic it was for me to meet him here. Then I pointed towards my car. He dragged his feet on his way to it. We plopped down in the front seats. Carla was the last person in that seat. His legs sat up high. He fiddled with the lever to push the seat back.

"Johnnie baby, my main man. What's happenin'?"

"You just gone keep fucking with me huh? I told you Jack, I don't know shit about no murder."

"Good thing I'm not here about a murder right now."

"Then what do you want?"

"Drop a dime on Reverend Brown. Everything you know about him. His son is missing and I need info on him. Does he have any enemies?"

"I still ain't talking to you," he said. I reminded him of my promise from earlier. A ten dollar bill dropped in his hand didn't hurt either. I decided on a different approach and figured paying him off would work better than threatening him. He began to sing like Stevie Wonder.

"He got a few enemies around here alright. The main one is this pusher that's about a street over."

"A pusher?"

"Yeah. All kind of folks come in and out. The Reverend didn't like it so he tried to run him out the neighborhood. I thought he wouldn't live another month doing that. I guess won't nobody kill a man of God."

"What's his name?"

"Was it James? Ron? No. Paul. I can't seem to remember. Maybe a few more dollars would jog my memory."

He dramatically rubbed his eyes.

"You little motherfucker. I'm empty right now."

"Well then I'm empty on information. But that kid don't deserve none of that. He was just too trusting though."

"What do you mean?"

"If he knew you, he'd take your word for anything."

"You don't say. Well look, I'll be back in the morning. They got a search party going on."

"Will you be back with more dough?"

"You little shit."

"Hey, don't talk to me like that anymore. Remember, you fucking need me asshole."

He opened the car door, hopped out and slammed it. Just like that, he crawled off to whatever hole he and his buddies came from.

With the last light in the sky I canvassed the neighborhood. Kids were all over the neighborhood getting the last of their outside time before another unforgiving winter. None of them knew where Junior was. He had gone to the park and played for about an hour. But then he had to leave and go to the store again. That was the last they had seen him. The boy ran away, and I didn't blame him for wanting to escape the Reverend. But I couldn't figure out why.

I was accustomed to long days but this one was different. A

lot had happened. I could have kept searching for this runaway now or go home and get some shut eye. I would've been more useful the next day if I went home.

I drove north on Van Dyke. The street was beginning to calm down. Shops were closing up and people were heading home. I slowed down when I reached the scene of the crime. The asphalt and curb still had the burn print of the police car. I could still smell the burning metal. I spoke out-loud.

"I'm gonna find you sons of bitches too."

I was well on my way to becoming police chief. Hell, maybe even the mayor.

That old man I shot in Vietnam left an impression on me. I shake when I think of the courage it took. He stood in front of an entire platoon. All hungry, tired and far from home. Thirsty for blood. Fingers on triggers, itching for revenge. And to say "shoot me and leave my village alone." "Leave my loved ones alone". That shit gave me chills.

What do you do to a man that was willing to die? That day I learned there wasn't much you could do. His mind was already made up. I should've sent that story to LBJ. Maybe then they would've seen what we were up against.

In the humblest of all places, a rice paddy. I saw what one man could do. I saw just how powerful one man could be. I saw what a leader was supposed to be. That was the bravest man I ever met. We needed a chief who was ready to die for his beliefs. We needed someone who knew the people and the city. Someone who could make the tough decisions and straighten this shit out. I was just the man for it.

I hadn't felt this excited since I was in that jungle. I noticed that Marvin was on the radio. I put the music on blast and glided all the way home.

11

Chapter 11

Sam Cooke was the greatest singer and song writer ever. His music had a way of easing my mind. I had to throw out several albums from playing them too much. Carla would threaten to take them out back and shoot them. She likes the new shit they play. Earth, Wind and Fire and all that. I guess it's cool, but there was only one other thing that eased my mind. Tasha sounded better than any Sam Cooke record.

I made it home. The scene was quieter than where I had just come from. A few kids screaming and playing but that was about it. Less cars, less ruckus. I walked through the front door and instinctively dropped my bag. Tasha and that goofy dog were spread out on the living room floor. Both were flat on their stomachs with their legs behind them. Muddy was the first dog I've ever seen do that.

The two of them hopped up and attacked me. Per usual, the three of us fell to the ground.

We lived in a pretty dope crib and were trying to fill the other two bedrooms with more kids. I could've even turned the maid's quarters on the third floor into a bedroom. Tasha was born a year after I got back Stateside. I hate to say it, but if it weren't for her, I don't think Carla and I would be together now.

Something changed between us when I got back. It's like the fire just went out. We used to go at it every day like rabbits. Now we barely touch each other. Don't get me wrong, she's a fox with a body better than Thelma. I just couldn't make any sense of it.

I didn't have any problems down there. Hell, I couldn't control myself when Chelle was around. Carla and I just lost it. She began to act different. She'd bring these horrible moods out of me. I tried not to think about it too much. Even when we did bang, I'd only do it to shut her up. Even then, I'd think about Chelle or Thelma.

We met at a dance. She went to Cass Tech and I went to Northern. Her family was like mine. "Uppity." We didn't just hear that from whites, but from other Negroes as well. Two working parents and speaking like you had some God damn sense was uppity then.

To be fair, there was a lot of uppity shit going on back then, especially with skin color. My mom's mother could've passed for one of them white kids that we laughed at while they danced on the Dick Clarke show. It must have bothered her because she married the blackest man she could find.

The law of the land was to hire blacks that were "light, bright and damn near white". Carla experienced that when she tried to work at Hudson's Department store downtown. I guess anyone too black would offend the white customers. The Urban League had taught her how to dress, what to say and even how to say it for the interview and they still wouldn't overlook her brown skin. Times were a trip back then.

I stopped dating Carla when I went off to war. She continued to date me though. I'd still write her damn near every day. She still has those letters. I read them once and nearly burned them. I don't even recognize the man who wrote that. The threat of dying was so prevalent that I guess it had a way of pulling them emotions right out of you. I bled all that bullshit out though.

Carla was there for all my night terrors. She even brought me the night light that sat in our room. I'm not proud to tell it but I can't be in the dark anymore. It brings back them memories. Rivers of blood. Sometimes the whole room would rattle. The explosions right in front of me. Worst of all, that damn ringing in my ear.

It was so bad that Carla would have to sing me to sleep. A soft song, just loud enough to drown out the ringing. Stand By Me by Ben E. King. Carla was a damn good woman. She passed the test from my mom, grandmas and aunts, and that's saying a lot.

She leaned up against the kitchen wall and smiled at me playing with Tasha.

"Alright, alright. Give your dad some space, I'm sure he's very tired."

I picked up Tasha and kissed her on the cheek. A studio audience laughed when I rubbed Muddy's head. I looked up at Good Times on the T.V.

"Uh, what are you doing little girl? You know the rules."

"Aw come on Dom. She did good on a spelling test today so I decided to let her watch something tonight."

"I don't care if she cured Legionnaire's. She can watch whatever she wants on the weekend."

"Don't be like that Dom, she earned it."

Carla wrapped her arms around me. I bent down to let her

kiss my cheek.

"How was your day?" she asked. Just like them old cartoons, I floated into the kitchen, pulled by the sweet smelling corn-bread.

I gave her the rundown of my day. The murder was all over the news. She had to have known but hearing it from me brought a different seriousness. She had been smiling before. But any talk of murder always hit her hard. Like I said, women witnesses always empathize and picture their loved ones. She was always worried something would trigger another night terror for me.

"How'd it go when you saw the uh, the body?" she asked.

I had been sitting at the counter chopping onions. I dropped it and looked over at her. The question was sincere enough. She looked scared to even ask it. Muddy sat at the door of the kitchen with his paw touching the yellow tile.

"Uh huh, nope, get the hell out of here," I barked at him. I scared the shit out of him. "Tasha come get him."

He dropped his ears and let Tasha lead him out of the kitchen like a toy and into the living room. Carla put the greens in a red Pyrex dish and stared over them. I think she wanted me to forget she asked.

"What do you mean?" I asked.

"Well, you know with all your-"

"With all my what?"

"You know Dom."

"No Carla, I don't know. Do I need to buy a vowel? Why the hell are you talking in riddles? Say what you gotta say."

She was afraid. Not physically. I'd never put my hands on her. But when I got going, it was hard to stop me. She never responded so I changed the subject. She gave a sigh of relief.

"Anyway, now I'm stuck on this case with this bullshit

Reverend."

"What would your mama say if she heard you curse a Reverend like that?"

"He ain't no real Reverend."

"Why do you say that?"

"Remember, when I first got back, those faggots had those little antiwar protests at the airport?"

"Yeah, but what's he got–"

"He's the one that set it up," I yelled.

"But why would a Reverend do that?"

"It ain't the first time he stuck his head in some shit. One of the neighborhood kids tells me he does the same over there."

"Is he trying to help?"

"You help by understanding what the fuck you're trying to help in the first place. He don't know shit about war but led a protest that almost started a riot."

"Come on Dom. I don't think that was his intention."

"It don't matter. Every bottle and fruit. Every hock of spit they hurled at us was because of him."

"Maybe–"

"He set it up," I interrupted. "Whenever you're top in command, whatever your troops do, you are to blame. It's that simple."

"But are you going to let that affect your case?"

"Of course not. I'm a professional. I won't let personal feelings in the way."

Her face screamed "bullshit".

"Dom, you hold onto a grudge better than any man I've ever met in my life. Remember Henry?"

"What about that bastard?"

"See? And that was only over ten dollars six years ago."

"That jive motherfucker shouldn't have taken the bread if he couldn't pay it back."

"But when will you let it go?"

"When I get my ten dollars back."

"What if you never get it back?"

"Then it will keep accruing interest."

She told me some long drawn out story about a Negro Doctor named Ossian Sweet. In the early 1900s, he brought a house over on the east side. Negroes wasn't supposed to be over there. Before they moved in, a mob of pecker woods gathered outside the house. They started throwing things at the house.

Little did they know, Old Dr. Sweet and his family inside had rifles. Someone took a shot and killed one of the white attackers. Strangely, a jury found him not guilty but his troubles had just started. Misery followed him. The stress built up and one day they find Dr. Sweet in a bathroom with a bullet in his head. I couldn't understand the relevance.

I had never heard of the Doctor. I needed to drive by. She looked disappointed when I asked where the house was. That woman knew me well. I assured her that any bullet I die from won't come from my gun. If people didn't do me wrong, I'd have no reason to hold a grudge right?

I asked how her day went out of a mere formality. I already knew. Connecting calls. Gossip. Out to lunch where Sophie complained about her drunk husband. Or Margaret showing off some new shoes. They never talked about shit that mattered.

I let her talk to get it out. My body was in the kitchen buy my mind was miles away. Chelle lived in the northwest in a Jewish neighborhood. I wondered what she was doing.

Carla finished ranting and I went out to the back porch to get some air. My little garden looked like no one had touched it in years. I refused to give up on it though. It just seemed to get worse and worse as the years went by.

I got some tomatoes out of it the first year but it was downhill ever since. Not even my mom and grandma could come over and get it right. The door opened behind me. Tasha and Muddy poked their heads out. I called her over to me.

"It's dying," she said.

I grabbed her and pulled her close to me.

"Yeah, I know."

"Why?"

"You don't let him pee in it do you?"

"No."

"Then I don't know baby. Let's just go eat."

12

Chapter 12

Only a fool puts his trust in a man who wouldn't take a bullet for him. Back in Vietnam, I trusted every last one of them Soldiers. Sometimes I trusted the dogs even more. Hendrix was my service partner. He took "man's best friend" to another level.

Dogs truly are our greatest allies. Horses might have been most useful, perhaps even more revolutionary but nothing replaces a dog. They have an almost sickening amount of loyalty. I gave Muddy that same amount of trust. He leaned his goofy head out of the passenger window as I cruised down Van Dyke with open lanes that Friday Morning. Riding through empty streets gave me a freeing feeling.

I guess the Reverend had some respectable things about him. Some of the tithing funds went to pay off medical bills. Many Negroes had problems paying their inflated mortgages and he appropriated church funds to help with that. I knew he was involved. But I never expected the mass of volunteers that braved that frosty October morning.

There was no place to park within a couple hundred feet. I

arrived late and tried to slip into the crowd unnoticed. The entire group stood in the vacant lot and huddled up in front of the Reverend. To his right were his daughters and wife. Behind him, the mural of Jesus held his hands out. I shook hands with the officers at the front of the crowd and watched the Reverend.

His pea-coat and hat ensemble didn't fit the occasion. He looked like he was speaking at a funeral. The power had begun to fade from his voice.

"Good morning brothers and sisters, uh, I will try my hardest to be brief."

He was anything but brief. He droned on and on. But not in his typical preacher fashion. He had lost a step. A chink in the armor. Normally quick witted and articulate, he stumbled over his words and rambled for quite some time. Eventually Deacon Jeremiah and that same scraggly looking white cat had to end his speech.

I felt bad for the man. The hair he had left was frazzled. It might not have seen a brush in a week. He looked to have just rolled out of the bed. That's not even the worst of it. Somehow, he managed to smell even worse today. I had to be twenty feet out when I caught a whiff of him. I cautiously shook his hand.

He thanked me for coming. His eyes lit up when he saw the K-9 units that I had arranged. He gave me his general search plan. As he did so, someone caught my eye.

At the back of the crowd was Johnnie Parlor. A hat tried its best to cover his mound of hair. He put his hands next to his face and rubbed his fingers together. I slipped through the volunteers to greet him.

"Did you bring enough people?" he asked.

"We'll find out."

"Y'all got the block real hot right now."

"Then it's best for everyone to help us. The quicker we find the boy, the quicker we get out of here. What you got for me?"

"It ain't much on the vine about them cop killers."

That was a lie. He knew who did it. Seventy five percent of the people here had to have known who did it. Unless they weren't from this neighborhood. He continued.

"But just stay cool. They gonna talk soon. They can't do something like that and not get the itch to tell people. They gonna have to blab about it to make a name for themselves and the case will break."

"And what about the boy?"

"What about my consultant fee?"

I handed him another ten dollars.

"Look, I hate talking to you. But I hate seeing a young brother missing. The Reverend don't have no shortage of enemies around here. It's a local pusher that they call 'Cyclops'."

"Cyclops?"

"Yeah. I'm only telling you about him cause he's a pusher and making zombies out of the community." He took a deep breath. "I ain't giving no names or addresses. You can look that up. But him and the Reverend got into it not too long ago."

"What was it over?"

"I ain't got all the details. The Reverend probably tried to do something about him pushing dope around here."

"And that's all you got? What does he look like? Where is he?"

"I ain't no pig, I don't work for you. I'm doing this out the kindness of my heart. I don't owe you shit."

I cursed him and immediately ran to a pay phone and called the office. Officer Hughes worked at the records department. He was my man. Luckily Cyclops had been picked up before and we had a file on him.

His name was Cyrus Edwards and he lived right down the street. He had been picked up a couple times, a few years before. I finally had a lead. Muddy picked up on my excitement as we walked to his house.

I expected to find a typical dope spot. Boarded up windows. Uncut grass leading up to a porch that was caving in on itself. But instead his home was one of the best kept houses on the well put together block. I wondered if we were in the right spot. Only a few leaves dotted the lawn.

Despite being a detective, I was confident that he would talk to me. I looked just like another searcher going door to door. I hopped up the green steps. The screen door rattled as I banged on it.

To my right, the blinds moved. I heard him putting on shoes. He came close to the door. I pushed back my jacket and readied my hand on my pistol. Just in case.

"Yeah, who is it?" his strong voice yelled out.

"A concerned citizen. Looking for a missing boy."

"Well you're at the wrong house."

"Come on Cyrus. I need your help."

It was silent for a moment after that. Without a doubt he weighed his options. He was a smart man and decided to open the door. A young, hip looking dark skinned cat stared at me through his right eye. The other eye was a cloudy, white color. Something like a glass marble. I stared into the good eye as I spoke to him.

"Cyrus Edwards?"

"Who's asking?"

I began to give my name and title. I couldn't say the word detective before he began to close the door in my face. I needed to flex on him a little.

"Cyrus, we got a file on you a mile long. I ain't here to arrest you, not yet. But you're gonna make it hard for yourself if you close that door." He hesitated. I threw in a couple shots to pump his ego just in case. "Your name been ringing in the streets. I'm just here for information on the missing boy. That's all."

Appeal to a man's ego and you can damn near control him. I see why women do it so often. A lot of these cats had this huge sense of importance. Like they were God's gift to the neighborhood. They wanted to be local celebrities and often were. The bluff worked like a charm. That door opened slowly.

"Hold on Jack, tie that fucking dog down there at the end of the railing," he said.

A simple request. I gave in and took Muddy off the porch. He always picked up on what I was thinking. He waited patiently.

"Why's a pig showing up at my door?"

He twitched his nose often, in a telltale sign of an addiction coming on. He buttoned up his shirt to his thin chest.

"You know about Wallace Brown's missing son?" I asked.

"I've heard about it."

"I'm sure you have."

"Man what you tryna say?" he shot back.

"I'm just asking the neighborhood what they known about the Reverend."

"I don't know nothing about him."

"Really? Cause word on the vine is that y'all don't get along too well."

"I ain't never spoke to him a day in my life."

I stared into that eye.

"My man, let's not make this difficult. The next answers you give me are gonna determine where your life goes."

I had to be firm. If you weren't, they'd never respect you. He spoke.

"Man, you trying to say that I had something to do with his kid?"

"I'm not saying anything Cyclops. Cyclops or Cyrus, which do you prefer?"

He didn't answer.

"It's just my job to ask questions."

"Look, ask all you need to but you ain't gone ever connect my name to some missing kids. You gotta be fucking jiving me right now."

"Give me a little background on the fight between you two. Everybody around here knows about it."

"Man, I ain't got to talk to you."

"Oh but you do. Believe it or not, I'm the best friend you got in that department right now. I'm the only thing stopping them from running in your house and kicking you while you're in handcuffs. Now I came here reasonable. Don't jerk me around."

"I swear you motherfuckers are dirty. Alright man, fuck. Yeah I know that two-bit pulpit pimp."

"What do you mean?"

"It ain't no different than most of them pastors. One day the motherfucker showed up on my porch. He all dressed up and stepping on my grass and shit like he owns the place. Kinda like you and that mutt."

I looked back at Muddy. He was ready to pounce. Cyclops continued.

"Some punk ass white boy banged on my door talking about the kingdom of God. Idolaters and kicking us out. It was a part of one of his 'Clean Up Your Act' days. I was about to shoot his ass until Brown came up. Him and some fake ass disciples go around telling us how to live. Do you mind?" he asked pulling out a cigarette.

He asked out of sarcasm. He lit it while asking the question. He blew the smoke out the open doorway.

"He saved that white boy that day."

"And that's why you all got into it?"

"They come around acting like they better than us. How were are ruining the community. You a white boy," he yelled. "You don't even live here and gone try to clean it up? I usually lay low. But I pulled my pistol on him. I think he pissed himself. I told them I would shoot the next mother fucker that walked past my house."

"A little harsh don't you think?"

"I was defending my home and this here neighborhood. They ran off. Screaming about how God was gonna get me back. Right after that, pigs began to drive by. It don't take no scientist to figure out who been calling."

"And how long ago was this?"

"Maybe two, three summers ago. Everybody around here loves me. I look out for everybody and they look out for me. We ain't had no problems."

"Wouldn't they look out for Brown too?"

"That's probably why he got beef with me. He wanna be top dog. He ain't shit, but it ain't worth taking a kid over. I don't touch kids Jack. I guess he finally pissed off the wrong cat then."

"Hmm, I guess so."

"You know what a motherfucker got to do to make me mad enough to grab a kid? That's some mafia type shit Jack. Some Vito Corleon shit. I'm talking big bread. I'd put my hands on him before I went after a kid."

"Then why didn't you?"

"My big cousin goes to his church. I try to avoid touching pastors if possible."

"But does that mean a pastor's kid is off-"

"Look Jack, I told you I ain't do nothing to no kid. Now you said you had questions and I answered. I ain't trying to been seen talking to you for too long, so unless you got something important to say, I'm closing the door."

"Okay be cool, be cool. Who else would have a problem with him around here?"

"The better question is who wouldn't? He called the pigs on some of the races just up the street on French Road just a few weeks ago. He's a nuisance Jack, and got a lot of enemies. Good luck."

The door slammed shut. Suspicion surrounded him. He didn't want to kill a Reverend so he did the next best thing. Maybe he was just trying to teach him a lesson. Something in the water wasn't clean.

I turned around and untied Muddy. When I was a kid, we had this little brown cat named Oscar. Mom and Pop would always make little voices for him. We have always talked to and for our pets. I can't explain it, it's just what we would do. I stared into Muddy's eyes. He was just as confused as I was. I spoke to him.

"I know bud. This thing is getting deeper than we thought."

13

Chapter 13

We got two seasons in Michigan, winter and construction, and construction season was coming to an end. We flipped what had to be thousands of rocks and trash can lids that morning looking for that kid. Every crack and crevice was investigated. We checked under cars and buses. In alleys and abandoned buildings. Ultimately, the search was called off a little after noon. Wherever he was, I hoped he was inside somewhere warm.

I made sure to keep walking by Cyclops' house. I could feel that one eye staring at me through the blinds. I had no evidence that linked him to Junior. But he did have the perfect motive. Even the capability.

But if it was him, he couldn't have done it without someone noticing. He's the neighborhood star. Someone would have seen it and spoken up right? I mean, even if he gave them some dough here and there, wouldn't they help a child? I began to wonder.

I dropped Muddy back off at home and went to meet Wendell and Chelle for lunch. I called off my lunch plans with Carla. I needed to be away from problems for at least an hour. All she would do was ask me some bullshit.

Wendell rarely left the office. He was a strange case. Sometimes I wondered if he was really a detective or not. Maybe Lieutenant was doing him a favor by giving him a job. He never really did anything. In any case, the three of us realized how important it was to stick together. We'd set up lunches once a week or so.

Our favorite spot was over near the Wayne State football stadium. It was a cozy little neighborhood with Victorian style homes that were packed together on top of each other. I walked inside the restaurant and greeted our favorite waitress, Nora. Her caked on makeup couldn't hide the years of stress and alcohol abuse. Underneath it, she was a nice lady. She pointed me to Chelle who sat alone by the window. Her delicate hand waved me over.

We had our own little language together. Sometimes I didn't even need to say anything. I got to the table and stood still. Our eyes locked. I shifted them to the door, then back to her again. She burst out laughing and stood up. She switched seats and put her back to the door.

"Oh yeah. I forgot you like to see the door in case some cat comes in looking for the bread you owe him right?" she smiled. Nora came over and took our orders.

"In this line of work, you never know," I said.

"Yeah, I guess you're right."

"Where's old man Dell?"

"He said he couldn't make it."

"Dell is a strange one sometimes ain't he?"

"You know something? As much as we go out to lunch, he never really talks about himself."

"Something happened that got him put behind a desk. I don't think he likes it too much."

"What do you mean, something happened?" she asked.

We went back and forth about Wendell. Born in North Carolina. That country boy had a hard time with the rigors of big city life. Imagine going through life walking. Then you move up north where everybody is running at 100 miles an hour. Poor country bumpkin probably couldn't handle it. She mentioned how Mitchells seemed stressed lately.

"Don't worry. He's at his happiest," I said. "It's deer hunting season."

Nora came over to us with our food. Chelle and I were too much alike. We would always order the same thing. The chicken salad for her and for me, the world famous burger and fries.

Carla always dragged me from place to place. She loved trying new things. Whether it was a restaurant or some bullshit hobby. Chelle and I saw eye to eye. We liked knowing what we were getting into. The routines gave me a safety net.

"Soon," I began with a mouth full of fries, "Mitchells will invite us to his cabin. We'll catch some deer and he'll forget all about the shit."

"You can't hunt. You a city boy."

We had this way of joking with each other. She knew how to press my buttons.

"If it runs on four legs, I can catch it. Been that way since I was ten years old."

"Is that so? Give me one funny hunting story."

I thumbed through the folders in my mind. The time I killed a huge buck? No, too standard. How about that boar that jumped up when we approached it? No. I had just the one. I took a deep breath and began my tale.

"My pop and grandad would always take me with them. They had a friend with a cabin up in Atlanta, Michigan. He'd let us use it from time to time. We'd be the only Negroes for miles and miles. But they both old school Negroes. Stronger than today's."

She shook her head in agreement.

"So this time, me and my pop are up there hunting some deer. We with about, six of our friends. We figure it's better to split into groups of two. So me and pop are treading light through the woods. Didn't wanna step on any sticks or anything."

"Cause it'll run off the deer?" she cut in.

"Exactly. They hear very well. We're going around and not finding anything. Pop sends me up a tree onto a platform to get a better view. So, I'm up there and don't see a God damn thing. But you gotta stay very still."

I took a bite of my burger. She hadn't touched her food. Her eyes were wide open as she waited for more of the story.

"It takes patience. My hands still shiver when I tell this story. I'm on that platform shaking like a runaway. Even with the gloves and warm gear I had on. But I'm trying to make an impression on pop so I struggled through it."

"What time of year was it?"

"Late January."

"Oh so it was cold, cold?"

"Better believe it. It had to be two hours without seeing anything. Then out of nowhere, two white boys showed up. They are probably three hundred yards from me talking to pop. This is 1961 I think? Oh the tension was in the air. They got their rifles in their hands."

"And they're right next to your dad?" she asked.

"As close as you to me. Now my pop is a hard ass. Rough.

107

Stubborn, but under it all, he's real social. Loveable. But them white boys are unpredictable. And pop is quick to tell one to kiss the blackest part of his ass. So I did what came natural. I took aim."

She finally began to eat but her eyes never left me. I was being very demonstrative with the story. In Vietnam we had to entertain ourselves. Other than the heroin, stories became a great pastime. I learned how to captivate. I continued.

"It was a boy and his daddy. Probably my age. I put my sights right on the dad's right ear. If I'm gonna lose my daddy, then he was too. Thirty seconds seemed like an eternity. Then, Pop remembered I was up there. Mind you, I'm rubbing the trigger the whole time. Waiting for the chance."

"And they are how far again? Two hundred yards?"

"Like three, give or take. I can hit a fly from there."

She smiled.

"So pop turned towards the tree. He threw his hands up and shouted. He was so loud, we didn't find one deer that day. He called me down there to meet them. They were from Battle Creek. They were some cool white boys."

"What did they say about it?"

"We all laughed it off afterwards. Hell, the boy said he would've done the same thing. That was the first time I almost blew a hole through someone's head."

Her expression changed.

"Well that wasn't funny at all," she said.

"Oh, yeah well I guess not, but it's my favorite."

"And you were really going to shoot his dad?"

"If they shot mine, hell yeah. Nobody messes with my pop," I shrugged.

We finished lunch and went back to the precinct. I made the

mistake of going to the bathroom. Symanski always seemed to pop up at the wrong moment. I got my rod in my hands and comes in talking. He left a vacant spot between us.

"Well, well, well, if it isn't Sherlock fucking Holmes."

I stared straight ahead at the wall. Proper piss etiquette.

"What are you bitching about now?"

"You know exactly what I'm talking about. You still been sniffing around my case."

"Man, don't talk to me with your damn pecker out."

I zipped up my pants and went to wash my hands. He turned his head towards me.

"You're out of order, Broddie, and you know it. That's why you won't look me in the eyes."

"I won't look you in the eyes cause I had my dick in my hands."

"No, my guy is already dead. That kid you're looking for might still be alive. But instead of going after him, you're wasting time looking at what I got going on."

That big mouthed store owner told him. Bastard.

"Look, Broddie, we have our differences. That's fine. But one thing that we can agree on is that-"

"No, you look. You don't know shit about the case I got. Ain't nothing happen to that boy. He's just running away from strict parents and that's all. Ain't nothing else to it."

I truly believed that. Sure, I was beginning to have my doubts. But I was positive he would turn up. I couldn't let Symanski know that though. Right on cue, the great Lieutenant walked in.

"I can't keep you two fags away from each other. After you're done blowing Symanski, head straight to my office, Broddie."

I couldn't catch a break. Wendell walked out of Mitchells'

office. I told him that Chelle had his food. He thanked me and walked by. What the hell was that about? Mitchells probably was getting on him too. He's a Nazi sometimes.

I sat down and waited for him. I was ten seconds away from turning that Marciano picture around. Mitchells waddled in to the room and plopped in his chair.

"Well?" he said.

I rubbed my face and sighed.

"You got an update for me?" he asked.

"Yeah, but it ain't much of a good one. This thing with Lyles is really giving me the fits."

"Lyles? You mean the Reverend's missing boy, right?"

"Oh yeah, what did I say?"

He gave me a stern eye.

"Yeah, well this thing with Brown is really giving me the fits. When I first got over there, everything was too perfect. It looked either like a cover up, or that he just ran away."

"Why do you say that?"

"The house was too perfect. Too clean. Even his room was perfect and that's unusual for a kid."

"Maybe they just keep a clean house?"

That was possible. Even white folks hire Negroes to clean their place. I wasn't buying it though.

"Maybe. At first, I'm thinking he ran away because of the pressure of being a preacher's kid. But one of my informants told about the Reverend and one of the neighborhood pushers. That didn't surprise me, he gets into it with a lot of people."

"Broddie," he said. His look grew even sterner. "Your personal feelings are getting in the way. Look, I hated them war protesting faggots just as much as you. But you have a job to do."

"Yes sir."

"Now tell me more about that pusher."

I gave him the run down on Cyclops. Height. Weight. Criminal history. Even how manicured his lawn was. I also told him about the store owner. He looked shocked to hear that the Reverend wasn't as well loved as he believed. He thought the Negro Reverend was God in the Negro community. And he was half right, but Brown wasn't like the other pastors.

"Maybe Cyclops takes kids and forces them to sell for him?"

"I'd sell my left nut if that was the case. They don't involve kids in dope like that. Even if they did, he'd have an overflowing list of applicants. He wouldn't need to take anyone."

"Well keep an eye on Cyclops and the store owner. The longer these missing persons cases drag, the harder it gets to find them alive."

"Yes sir."

The next twenty-four hours flew by in a bit of a blur. I know I went home. But I can't remember any of the conversation with myself and the girls.

All I remember from home is the Reverend calling me a few times. I told Carla to ignore it. He had to have called twelve times. He was damn near in tears the first time I picked up. I couldn't listen to some grown man cry. I had a boy to find.

I spent most of my time going door to door. Fifteen people opened and spoke to me. Countless others didn't and told me to fuck off. I came to one general consensus. While the Reverend did mean well, he was in fact, a "two-bit pulpit pimp". Or at least he used to be.

I heard more about him than I was comfortable with. His exploits with women outside of his wife. The gambling den he used to run. He had the sweetest moonshine in the city. The problem was his mouth. He got in trouble with some white gangsters back in the day and that's when he flipped the script and opened his church.

I don't know if I believe that. I certainly had my problems with him. I had been shot at. Stabbed. Punched. Kicked. But the only time I was ever spit on was at his antiwar rally. I'm coming home from protecting our country and I got fucking spit on. Through all the hatred for him, a man wouldn't try to pimp God, would he? Could he? But then again, why would they lie about it?

It was late that next afternoon. I was one of the last ones in the office. I could hear that damn ringing in my ear. I wondered if it would ever stop. I had some of Cyclops' files on my desk. The old folks always said that you reap what you sow. According to my research, the Reverend had done a lot of sowing. Maybe this was a part of his reap. My desk phone began to scream at me.

"Detective Broddie speaking."

"Oh my God, Dom."

Carla was frantic. She stumbled over her words and was nearly out of breath.

"Carla, slow down, what's wrong?"

"What did I tell you about grabbing Tasha from school and not telling anybody? Put her on the phone."

Carla never was this demanding with me.

"What are you talking about? I haven't done that since the last time. I don't have her. Where is she?"

The phone began to slip in my palm. A million thoughts raced through my mind.

"Oh my God Dom...The school said they thought you came and got her."

"No, no, no, no, d...did you call your parents?"

"They didn't have her. I even called yours and they don't either."

"Meet me at her school. I'm headed there now."

Chapter 14

I had run from artillery shells. Seen men blown to pieces right in front of me. But none of that could prepare me for this. I fumbled with the phone as I spun out Pop's number on the rotary. I slapped the desk each time that it rang.

"Hello?" his voice said.

"Pop, did you or mom pick up Tasha from school?"

"No. What's wrong? You don't know where she is?"

I had to be trapped in a dream land. I had fallen asleep at my desk. My greatest fear was playing itself out. If I could just pinch myself, I would have woken up. I continuously did just that. The skin was rubbed raw. Each time I became painfully aware of just where I was and how real the situation was.

Pop's answer broke my heart. I slammed the phone down and grabbed my things. I flew down the steps. I must have looked like a madman. I ran and cursed all the way through the parking lot.

Of course, traffic seemed unusually heavy for it being that late in the evening. I cursed God with every name in the book. I didn't work but five minutes from Tasha's school but I swear the trip took fifteen.

I screeched onto the street and found Carla standing outside. Her hands were covering her mouth. Two officers and school faculty stood around her. I jumped out and ran full speed to them. I tossed my arms around her.

"What the fuck is going on?" I asked. I balled my fist up.

Ms. Byrd was the principal. She was old school. Never smiled. A no nonsense type woman. I wondered how something like this could have happened under her watchful eye. She talked like a typical politician.

"Uh, Mr. Broddie there is no easy was for us to tell you this but, and I do terribly apologize but we haven't been able to locate where Tasha is at this moment."

I flew to open my mouth. She was quick.

"But, but, but, we are looking for her at this very moment. As soon as the problem was realized, we called the police and took the proper steps to remedy the situation."

"Don't give me all that political bullshit," I barked at her.

"Now, Mr. Broddie, we need to -"

"What do you mean you don't know where she is? We dropped her off at the school this morning. That means she's in your care until she is picked up. That's how this shit works right?"

"Mr. Broddie please, we are doing everything we can-"

Carla stepped in.

"Janet you aren't doing everything you could. If you were, you would know where the fuck our daughter is. How the hell does a seven-year-old child just disappear and no one knows anything about it?"

Ms. Byrd gave a bewildered look. She turned to Tasha's teacher, Mrs. Truxton. I liked her when we first met. She was young, pretty and had a good head on her shoulders. As I stared at her then, the urge to wrap my hands around her neck rose. This was all her fault. She wiped her eyes and smeared her eyeliner.

She gave us all the minute details of the day. What the students ate for breakfast and lunch. Even the conversations between the six and seven year olds. She decided to take the kids out to play. Her reasoning was that winter would be there soon. It was best to get them outside one last time.

Tasha walked right by her on the way to the playground. Some little shit had tried to trip my baby, that's why she remembered it. They ran around playing and enjoying themselves. One of the parents came to Mrs. Truxton around dismissal time.

And do you know what they talked about? A God damn TV show. Nothing of substance. Nothing that mattered to the fucking world. My God damn daughter was gone because of a TV show. I fumed.

Officer Jamie Simons stood off to my right side. He could feel my energy. Thank God he moved closer. I don't know what I would've done.

No one took more pride in my job than Carla. On a daily basis, she flaunted it around. She threatened that school with the entire wrath of the police force. She even threw in the National Guard. We wouldn't need all that. One pissed off father was enough.

Ms. Byrd began to try to calm us down. Her use of words such as "dedicated" and "devastation" made me cringe. Her fake ass education annoyed me. She preached on the school being a family. With Tasha being one of their brightest stars. As she bullshitted us, a realization hit me. It couldn't be a coincidence.

"It's the same guy Carla," I said. I stared at the school's huge lawn. My body felt numb and for the first time, realized that I had left my jacket in the car. The wind bit my arms. Carla turned to me with a horrified expression.

"Dom, what guy?"

I didn't answer. The Reverend's son really was missing. And the son of a bitch who took him was toying with me. I immediately thought of that one eyed bastard.

"The guy, the, the guy who took the Reverend's son. It has to be the same guy. This ain't no coincidence."

We were wasting our time there. My body began to sway. I still felt like I was in a daze. I needed to move so I jogged around the school's enormous grounds. Then I went out to the neighborhood. I called out to God again and begged him to wake me up. But He don't listen to me anymore.

Everyone else followed suit. We ran door to door and our voices ran through the early twentieth century neighborhood. Carla and I were standing on a porch, pleading with a young couple for information when I heard my name. I turned and looked towards the street. Fifteen police cars now surrounded the school.

Mitchells was parked at the curb. He stepped out of car and flicked a cigarette on some fallen leaves. He surveyed the scene and locked eyes with me. I knew that look as well. He was fed up. Just like Lyles' murder, he took this one personal.

As I went down the steps, I reminded myself of my strength. Men like us believed in power. To be as stoic and statuesque as possible. Anything other than that was sissy shit. Even with a missing child, I had better hold it together.

I motioned for Carla who joined us. Mitchells began to talk. Behind him, people gathered on their porches and watched us.

I stared at everything except into his judging eyes. He wasn't the sympathetic type.

"Broddie, Mrs. Broddie, I, I'm so very..." He cleared his throat and fixed his tie. "I will spare no expense to bring her back. You both have my full support."

I remained silent. Not because I didn't know what to say. I had plenty to tell him. I just didn't want my voice to crack as I did so. Instead, I just shook my head at him.

"Any amount of officers. It doesn't matter. Cars, dogs, guns, men, you got it. We are going to get her back. Wendell will take the lead. You might not think much of him now, but he was once a very capable detective. He'll-"

"Dell?" I questioned.

"Yes. For the past few years he's been less than stellar but recently he's-"

My throat was on fire. I swallowed.

"No, no, no Lieutenant. I, I'm, I'm gonna work this case." Carla jumped in.

"Dom, I think you should just-"

"No, no, no. She's my daughter and I'll find her," I yelled at them. "I was already looking for one kid and now I got some more motivation to find the son of a bitch."

"You think they're related?" Mitchells asked.

"Of course they are. He knows I'm looking for him."

"Do you think it's Cyclops?"

"I don't know. But we'll shake him down too."

"Well Broddie, I think this case might be a little too close to home-"

"Lieutenant, what would you do if Ally was missing?" He didn't answer. Without a doubt, his granddaughter's face flashed in his mind. "My little girl is wondering where her dad is."

I couldn't help it but my voice cracked. I pictured her caged up like some animal. The thought alone made my skin crawl.

"She's not sitting up wondering when Dell will kick the door in. She's looking for her daddy."

I reluctantly wiped my eye and hoped no one noticed.

"Dom, I understand all that. But you won't think rationally about this. You know as well as I do."

"I've been in more stressful situations than any other detective. You know that more than anyone. This is a search and rescue mission. I'm staying on this case. And you know what? You can fire me for insubordination. But you won't stop me from working on this case and finding her."

Mitchells sighed and fished in his shirt for another cigarette.

"Good God son. Alright. What do you think we're dealing with here?"

He said how this isn't common with Negro children. Especially not in Detroit. The word "predator" slithered out of his mouth. Just the mention of it made me itch. I wanted to shoot something as soon as I heard it.

I couldn't even respond to it. Mitchells ordered all but two of the patrols to stay and the school. He told them to search ten square miles if they had to. Meanwhile, we left to search our home for clues. I ran up the steps and pulled my keys out.

All my tranquil breathing techniques did nothing. We stood there for at least a minute. I couldn't even steady my hand enough to unlock the door. Everyone was probably too embarrassed for me to say anything.

Finally, I got the key inside and snatched the door open. I screamed out her name. No response. Muddy came around the corner and matched my mood. He somehow knew that something was wrong.

I knew the procedure. We stood still in the middle of the living room. Officers moved around us like we were ornaments. Carla squeeze my hands so tight that I felt my circulation giving out.

I could deal with them dirtying our house. I could deal with them tossing things aside. I could even deal with tracking dirt. But I nearly lost it when they began to push our couch back. On top of that, they opened up a hallway closet. One even peaked under the dining room table.

The one who looked under the table was a brother named Scottie. I went to scold him but Carla beat me to it.

"Do you really think she would be fucking hiding from us? She's our God damn daughter."

I echoed her. It was so insulting to have officers check if your missing child was actually hiding in a hall way closet. Once Carla got going, it was hard to reel her back in."

"She went missing at school, not here. So why the fuck would you be looking behind a couch?"

Scottie didn't know what to say.

"Does it look like she can fit behind there?" Carla began to yell.

"Look, Dom, Mrs. Broddie, these are just precautions. You know how this goes." He stood up straight and grabbed his note pad. "I mean nothing by it Dom. I'm just doing my job. But we do need a detailed description and a photo of her."

Carla gave him more than he wanted. I thought that Tasha and I were closer than her and Carla but I stood there and listened to her give information on my daughter that I didn't even know. Her exact height and weight. Even the mole on the left side of her forehead. He jotted down every last detail about her.

Mitchells had been outside with a cigarette. I could see him through the blinds. He was first on my shit list. When he stepped inside, he took all the good air.

"Broddie, we have to take off. We've got everything we need."

I turned to the door and stared through him.

"I'm still on this case, Mitchells. I'm gonna be the one to find her."

"I understand Broddie, but you need help."

"I don't need shit."

"This ain't the time for you to play Billy Badass. This is about those children. Now this thing is getting bigger and I don't want any more to come up missing. I'm putting another set of eyes on this."

I hated to admit it, but he was right. The county north of us had been dealing with kids that turned up missing. Their bodies had been found several days later.

By then our families showed up to the house and crowded into the home. Carla nearly collapsed and disappeared into her father's gargantuan arms. Our mothers were equally overly dramatic about the little things. For something of this magnitude, they just cried with their faces in their hands.

Loud and expressive, I had a hard time relating to her father. If he loved something, he'd show it. If he wanted to hug you, he'd do it. Years of manual labor built him into a wall, even at nearly fifty years old. He open his arms and pulled me into the hug as well.

"Dear Heavenly Father, whose merciful name," he began. His voice had to have rattled the deer heads I had mounted on the basement wall. Everyone bowed their heads in solidarity with our spiritual leader.

Mitchells and the other officers excused themselves of the somber scene. I could hear their muffled voices as they went down the steps. They were probably talking shit about me. Blaming me. What father doesn't know where his own child is? What kind of father can't protect his daughter? I just knew they were blaming me for all this.

I didn't have a description, a witness, a trail, nothing. How the fuck does someone just vanish? Our families packed the den. They all brainstormed on what to do to find her. Whether it be search parties or calling Floyd Kalber from NBC.

Every Negro family has a Richard Pryor. My cousin Louie did his best to lighten the mood. The voices of Louie, Uncle Chuck, Aunt Barbara and more filled our house but everything felt empty without her. By now, I'd be coming home. Her and Muddy would jump on me. Carla would yell and tell her to pick up a toy or go get washed up for dinner. I could still hear her feet patting the floor as she ran through the house.

I stood in the kitchen bracing against the sink while my mother gave me every scripture she could think of.

"All things work together for good to them that love God, to them who are the called according to his purpose." She cradled my face in her hands as the words came out. Her thin arms wrapped around me. "God gives his toughest tests to his strongest soldiers. You'll find her baby, I believe it." She turned and went to the living room to pray with Carla's mother.

God wouldn't put my child through some bullshit for some "purpose", I thought to myself. He'd be one cruel son of a bitch if He did. Her words meant well, but feel short of the mark.

I watched my father. He was stoic in the dining room in his favorite rattan chair. He leaned on his cane in deep thought. He never said much and didn't need to. I needed some instruction. How would he handle this?

It wasn't my fault. I had been at work. He knew that I would do anything to protect my family. Tasha was rarely out of my sight. It wasn't my fault. He had to have known that.

He looked over at me. It was like I was staring at my future self. My eyes must have begged for advice. His mouth stayed shut. He nodded his head and gestured towards outside.

I walked to the kitchen doorway and looked at Carla. For the first time in years, I could feel what she was going through. Our grief tethered us and weighed heavy on me. A hopeless feeling of despair came with it. My stomach began to fight the rest of my insides. I was five seconds from throwing up. I leaned over the sink and spat.

Once I regained myself, I walked past everyone. I could feel their stares. All conversation in the house stopped but I didn't care. I ignored them all and went up to Tasha's room. I grabbed a sock and dirty shirt and walked back downstairs.

Their eyes still escorted me. Muddy jumped up when I grabbed his leash off the wall mount. At least one soul in there understood me. He knew where we were going. If I knew him like I think I did, he probably wondered what was taking so long. I looked back at everyone.

"Stay close to the phone in case anyone calls."

"Where are you going?" Carla said with tears in her eyes.

"To find our daughter."

15

Chapter 15

I can't remember if the street lights were out or maybe I just wasn't paying attention. I do know my breath spiraled up every time I breathed. I said another prayer. I asked God to at least let her be somewhere warm. He'd at least listen to that kind of prayer.

I used stories of the old heads to give me motivation. My grandpa on my pop's side, was known as one of the strongest men down in Hazelhurst, Georgia. The story goes that my grandma was walking back home from the store when a white boy spotted her alone and propositioned her. She politely declined and kept walking.

Well he didn't take kindly to that and followed her in his car, raising the amount of money each time. The encounter made her so uncomfortable that she dropped her groceries and ran. She crossed the railroad tracks back to the Negro side of town.

She tried to hide the encounter from my grand pop. That only made him angrier. He snatched a shotgun and marched right over to the man's farm the next day. He found him sitting on a rickety porch with his son drinking some tea.

Grandpa was black. And I mean black, black. His skin was lovely.   Imagine a six foot four, two hundred fifty pound, shotgun wielding Negro marching to your door. The white boy sent his son inside. He didn't want his boy to see him piss his pants.

My grandpa said if he ever so much as even looked at another Negro woman over there again, he'd answer to him. The white boy knew that "answer to him" meant him, and one hundred other angry Negroes just like him.

Needless to say, granny never had any problems walking to and from the store again. Those stories offered me the guidance that I needed. They taught me how to move. Grandpa would've marched outside and looked for Tasha. Hell, he might've even found her already. I came from that same cloth. I marched with a purpose.

The lights along Linwood Avenue snapped me out of my daze. I made it to the payphone about a block away. I dialed the number. A man in a blue Chrysler flew by me. I wondered what the biggest problem in his life was. A lost wallet? Maybe he couldn't pay a bill? I would've given my left arm to trade problems with him. The voice finally picked up the phone. He sounded weak.

"Reverend?"

"This is he, who is calling?"

"It's Detective Broddie. I, I have some news."

"Oh God, no, no, don't-"

"No, I'm sorry. It's not on Junior yet. We are still looking. But whoever did it has struck again and-" I couldn't get the words out. "But, now my daughter is gone. Earlier today. The son of a bitch took her right from school. Whoever took Junior knows I'm looking for him and took her."

125

"Jesus Christ Detective, I'm so sorry. So, who do you think it was?"

"I'm looking at..."

I didn't want to tell him about Cyclops. Knowing the Reverend, he'd march right over there. He'd ruin everything I was learning.

"I have two suspects Reverend."

"Who son?"

"I can't disclose that."

"These are dark times, Detective. I've been calling your home and office. We're doing another search in the morning. Please, you and your wife come and we'll find her as well. Detective," he said.

"Yes, Reverend."

"You're a father just like me. We have to find our babies."

"Yes sir Reverend. We'll be there first thing in the morning."

I slammed the phone on the receiver. I walked the ten minutes to Tasha's school. Inside my jacket pocket, I rubbed the pistol's trigger. Someone had to pay for this. And I was looking for a reason that night.

I walked to the side door where her teacher said they came out of at the end of the day. Muddy sat and prepared to clock in. I grabbed his big head and rubbed it. I whispered encouragement in his ear.

"Alright boy, let's do it again. We gotta find Tasha. Let's bring her home, I know you miss her too."

I pulled her shirt out of my pocket. Muddy took long whiffs of it. Labradors are the best dogs in the world. We used them in Vietnam. A good seasoned dog would find anything. A good seasoned tracker could tell you how many enemies, male or female and how tall. I had a perfect tracking device with me. His nose surveyed and then swept the ground like a minesweeper. I followed him to the swing set. Okay boy, she was here.

He led me over to the fence line. Why the hell would she have walked over here? Someone had called out to her. He led her to the fence line. Muddy continued and ultimately landed right at the curb. Some son of a bitch's car left oil spots here. Maybe it was old and beat up. That in itself was a clue. Muddy continued to sniff and toss leaves off the curb. Then, I saw a small red bow hidden among the leaves.

I grabbed that stupid dog and kissed him. He knew it was hers.

"I knew it you good mutt you." I spoke out loud to Tasha, wherever she was. "We're close baby girl. You are so smart." I turned back to Muddy. "She dropped this on purpose you know? She was here. The car was right here."

To my side, a door creaked. The man had been trying to open it slow. A voice came from it. I looked up at the house across the street like a deer in headlights. An old man stared at me. He did a poor job of hiding the shotgun.

"What the hell are you doing in front of my house?" he demanded.

"Sir, I was with the search party earlier."

"You were looking for that little girl?"

"Yes sir, that's my daughter. This is her bow. Did you see any strange cars or anything at your house earlier today?"

"I'm sorry to hear that son." He set the shotgun down behind the door. Thank God. "No, I didn't see anything. But then again, I wasn't looking for anything."

"I understand."

"But my daughter works night shift down at the hospital. She was up and at them during the day. I can ask her when she gets in tomorrow"

"I'd really appreciate that. Here's my card. Please give me a call when she lets you know something."

"Will do son. God bless you."

"Have a good night."

I wanted to offer him a blessing back. I was afraid it would come off strange and insincere.

From there, Muddy and I walked back to my house to get my car. A strange feeling came over me. There was a small, glimmer of hope, having found her bow. But there was an overwhelming sense of rage.

Muddy and I hopped in the car. I didn't plan on visiting my top suspect but I found myself sitting outside his home. The lights in the living room were on.

I opened my car door. My hand still tightly clutched the pistol. I struggled to take it off. My footsteps were light and soft as I toed up to the home. I crept around back where I heard voices. Laughter. Loud, boisterous howling that echoed in the night. I knew those sounds. A good game of spades was going on. Bottles clanged together and confirmed the good time they were having.

I put my back against the house and listened to the conversation. General bullshit banter. Who's dating who. Talking shit about how much money someone had.

I wrestled with myself for a moment. Grandpa had walked right up to the man and confronted him. He'd be disappointed if I didn't. I stood up straight and went around to the front door. The screen door was silent as I opened it slowly.

My heart raced. One false move and they'd know I was there. He'd come out blasting. Good luck explaining this to Mitchells. Then I heard a noise coming from my car.

I turned to see Muddy losing his mind in the back seat. He pawed at the window. His screams and cries were muffled by the closed windows. Maybe he wasn't so stupid after all. I knew what he was telling me.

I closed the door and made my way back to the car. I hopped in and rubbed his head. I thanked him and promised that we'd get him another way. He might have saved my life.

By the time I got home everyone was asleep. Carla laid on the living room couch faced down in the pillow. I grabbed the crocheted cover off the back of it and laid it gently over her. I dropped down to the floor under her and did my best to sleep. I still hoped this had all been a bad dream.

16

Chapter 16

It's next to impossible to sleep not knowing where your child is. It was hard sleeping when she was at her grandparents' house. She had to sleep somewhere wondering where I was. Parents protect and prepare their children for the real world. That's it. Prepare and Protect. I couldn't protect Tasha and I was a failure because of it. She slept God knows where with one question. "Where's daddy?"

My God it was miserable. Carla cried even in her sleep. I kept telling myself to "grab her you idiot. Get up on the couch with her and hold her. Something." I tried my best. All I could muster was to put my hand on her and rub her back. It might not have seemed like much, but it was the best I had.

There wasn't no point in laying around like we were sleep. We got up before the sun and woke everyone else up and got dressed. I didn't say much to Carla. I didn't have much to say. I didn't blame her for what happened. It wasn't her fault either.

On a normal morning she'd put on that Stevie Wonder. She'd sing her heart out. Tasha would join in singing about things she knew nothing about. I asked her what a "Village Ghetto

Land" was. She stared at me like I was speaking Vietnamese.

It was silent that morning. Usually the music annoyed me in the morning. For the first time that, I longed for it.

I immediately went to the phone and called Wendell. My heart dropped when he told me he didn't have any information yet. A part of me was glad that he hadn't found her. Not that I wanted him to fail, but I wanted me to be the one to succeed.

We went through the motions and everyone hopped in their cars. Muddy hopped in our backseat. I started my car and we pulled off. Carla laid her head against the window. I thought to myself, say something to her, anything.

"Don't worry. We're gonna find her," I said.

She turned her head towards me. Still leaning against the window.

"Don't worry? Don't worry. Where did she sleep last night Dom?"

I stayed silent.

"How did we let this happen?" She threw her hands over her face. Tears poured from between her fingers. I never knew what to say or how to behave in these situations.

"I..It wasn't us Carla, we are doing our jobs."

I didn't even believe that and she knew it.

"Then why isn't our baby at home? I don't feel like I did my job."

I couldn't answer that. I focused on the road and looked behind at the caravan that followed us. She continued.

"Maybe if I had done more research on the school, or, or, maybe if I showed up a little earlier to pick her up. I knew we shouldn't have moved over here. I fucking knew it."

Muddy did something I had never seen him do. He lowered his head and sympathized with her despair. It was usually only me or Tasha who could do that to him. But this time, I had just the words.

"Well why stop there? Maybe if we had her a year earlier. Or maybe if I didn't go to Vietnam. How about this, maybe if you had become a secretary instead, things would be different."

She was silent.

"Carla there's a million and one fucking possibilities that could have changed shit. But don't none of it matter right now. All that matters is finding her."

Silence.

"My baby is smart. She knew I would be looking for her. She dropped this for a clue."

I pulled Tasha's bow out of my pocket. Carla ripped it from my hand and clutched onto it.

"Do you really think we'll find her?" she asked.

"We'll find her. I've found people under worst circumstances than this."

"You can't shoot your way out of this Dom."

"Carla, we'll find her."

She grabbed my hand. I nearly pulled back.

"Okay but Dom, I can't do this alone."

"What?"

"Last night. You just left for the entire night. You didn't tell me or anybody else where you were going or when you'd be back."

"One, you weren't alone. Two, I told you I was going to look for her."

"Dom you left when I really needed-"

"You're fucking kidding me."

"We're supposed to be a team and-"

"You're really making this about you right now?"

"No, it ain't about me. It's about us and—"

"I really can't believe you. My daughter is missing and don't shit else matter to me but that. Not how you feel. Not holding fucking hands. And definitely not your fucking emotions. Finding our daughter is what matters."

I had begun to yell. Typically, Carla was mild mannered. I liked that about her. But she began to return the favor. I never liked a loud, yelling woman.

"It's about us. If you could shut your fucking mouth and listen for once you'd understand that. Our daughter is missing. Not yours, not mine, she's ours. I carried her for nine months not you."

I swallowed my words. She kept yelling at me.

"I need a husband. Not some roommate who can't even hug me at night when I'm sad over our daughter."

She continued to emphasize the word "our". I never noticed it. I always called Tasha my daughter. Carla just held her for me.

"So that's what you think huh?" I said.

"You're God damn right. For years I've done everything to and for Dominique. Back in high school when your daddy didn't come to your games? You was too proud to show that it hurt. Who was there? Me. I held you in my arms when you were having flashbacks. I brought you that fucking night light. I—"

I got real stern then. Women were good for that. Make you confided in them, then throw it in your face.

"I told you. Don't you use that shit against me."

"I'm not. I'm saying that I've been down for you since we met. Whenever you needed a shoulder, you had mine. Well when I need one, you can't be there for me?

I remained silent.

"Just cause you got a gun and can curse somebody out don't make you a good fucking husband."

She slumped down in her seat. The words were mumbled but just loud enough that I could hear them. They hit hard. But she couldn't know that.

"Man, you're wasting your breath talking to me. I'm on my way to find my daughter. You can yell about little bullshit that don't matter all you want."

Rouge Park was on the far west side of the city. 1300 acres of city land that was purchased back in the 20s. With playgrounds, swimming pools and even DPD's gun range being there, the park had it all, but the city's decline had begun to reach it to. Larger than Central Park, with some areas still resembling the forest that once sat there, it was the prime place to search for missing children.

We met in a large parking lot in the middle of the park. It didn't take long for the lot to fill up. The amount of people doubled from the first search. The media picked up on the cases. I hated all the attention. But it especially comforted Carla to see the city band together for the children. This city really can surprise me sometimes.

Reverend Brown, our families and I stood in front of the large crowd. Carla's grip cut the circulation from my hand. The space cadet white boy stood next to Deacon Jeremiah. They took turns speaking to the crowd. I grabbed Brown's attention.

All the blood in his body looked to have concentrated in his eyes. His hair sat in an untidy mess. And of course that rancid smell. Even in that early morning chill, it attacked my nostrils. My stomach tried to dance away.

I introduced him to my and Carla's parents. Things were

going well so far. So of course, my mother decided to ruin it. She stared deep into the red of Brown's eyes. I assume she found what she had been looking for.

"Are you alright Reverend?" she asked. "You don't look so good."

"Well, since you mention it, I'm not feeling my best. I'm sure you can imagine why."

My mother shook her sympathetic head. I searched for a way out of the conversation.

"I gave a sermon yesterday and for the first time, my strength failed me. It's hard to believe but I look better now, than I did yesterday."

"Well," my mother said. What was to come next was a story. I needed to intervene. I pulled Brown off to the side and told him I needed a word with him.

"Reverend I have something to tell you. Don't go off and do anything drastic because you'll jeopardize the investigation."

"What is it?" he begged.

"My number one suspect is Cyrus Edwards."

"No, not Cyrus?" he yelled.

"Keep your voice down."

"Then let's go get him now."

"I can't. I don't have evidence or a motive. He told me about the two of you."

"Yes, but I didn't imagine that he would ever do something like this."

"We don't know that he did it. We suspect. I hear he pulled a gun on one of the men in your program?"

"Yes. Brother Steven over there."

He pointed to the white space cadet and yelled out to him. He had a weird bounce in his step. He bopped over towards us. He pulled his bangs from in front of his eyes. We made our introductions.

"Steven, what happened with Cyclops?"

"We were just going door to door to get people to clean up the community. I had been walking with the good Deacon. I guess he didn't dig another brother telling him to clean up. We got into an argument and out of nowhere, the guy pulls a fu... excuse me, he pulled a pistol on me."

The anger was still fresh. It left an impression on him. With that much raw emotion, he was telling the truth.

"I did the Christianly thing and turned the cheek. Luckily Reverend Wallace came down to save me or I don't think I would've made it out of there."

My conversation with the Reverend and Steven was brief. That ended their contact with Cyclops. He didn't think Cyclops were capable of taking a child. I wasn't so sure.

Brown went up in front of the crowed. He closed his eyes and tilted his head up towards the grey sky. Somehow, he mustered up some strength. His eyes brightened when he opened them. That strength gave him poise and renewed his voice.

Was he really just a "two-bit pastor pimp?" At that moment, he looked and sounded just like a man of God. I wasn't sure of anything anymore. I found myself praying more. Trouble can have that effect on a man.

Brown weaved a speech of love and power. Of redemption and how the will of God can bring the best out of any man. The crowd exulted and erupted in applause. I got caught up in the hysterics as well. In the midst of me clapping, he pulled me up in front of him to speak.

I could hunt down soldiers in a jungle. I could jump out of a plane. I had even shot men who didn't deserve it as they begged for mercy. But standing in front of a crowd froze me. But that's what future police chiefs did right? Like that little Vietnamese man in the village, I wanted to lead. I stared into the trees and grass behind the crowd.

"Good morning, uh family," I said. They echoed. I gave my name, position and a little background on Tasha. As they shook their heads along with me, I gained confidence. I held up the flyer with her face on it.

"We believe that whoever took Wallace, also took Tasha. My wife and I have showered our baby with love from the day she was born. She is the sweetest little thing. She has this laugh that, that snatched me out of dark places. Oh, and she loved to ride on my back. You gotta see her and her dog. He's like her brother. She's the picture of innocence. At age seven she knows what college she wants to go to."

Some smiled while others held back tears. Something slid down my face. It was cold. It had to have been a rain drop.

"At seven, she already knows she wants to go to school at Michigan State. I just...please let's add her to the search. My baby didn't deserve this."

Deacon Jeremiah tapped me on the shoulder. I turned to see him and Steven staring at me. I guess they didn't get the memo. They hugged me. It was stiff and awkward. The two hugs I received in the past twelve hours were the only times I had ever hugged men. I had never even hugged my daddy. Him and grandpa just weren't them kind of men.

Jeremiah released me and began to take back control of the crowd. Seconds later everyone began to disperse. My mother pulled me aside.

"They oughta call him Reverend Brown Liquor. Does he always smell like that?"

"Not now mom," I said. I looked over to my dad. "Can you get her Pop?"

"I'm just saying," she continued. "He ain't gonna get much searching done like that."

Three hours flew by. Voices became soft and hoarse. The hopeful energy that we started with was fading. We hadn't found a damn thing. Which was somewhat of a good sign.

I came across a bum in the park. He had an elaborate tent set up. He looked suspicious, so I tossed his meager belongings around. What was strange was that he didn't put up a fight. Almost like he was used to being abused like that. He kept his cool as Muddy sniffed him down. Desperation made me violate an innocent man. I'm not a monster so I gave him two bucks and apologized.

The longer we searched, the more agitated I became. Far behind me, my mother walked with Carla. She recited scriptures that I didn't even know about. Eventually I tuned her out. They weren't helping.

I had been standing on a bridge. I stared off into the Rouge River for any sign or movement or disturbance in the flow. About one hundred yards off I saw something. I tossed a rock in the water next to it. My heart resumed normal operations when it was revealed to be just a stick.

I leaned on the metal railing of the bridge. The bitter cold of it stung my hands but I just didn't care. More hopelessness fell over me. Tires screeching woke me up. They had to be a quarter of a mile off. I thought nothing of them at first.

Then they screeched again. But this time they were much closer. Who the hell would be racing at a time like this? The engine came closer. I began to jog back towards Carla and the family.

I might have been two hundred feet away when a tan car slid around the corner. It struggled to control itself as smoke spiraled up from the burn marks it left. I cocked the hammer on the pistol and pulled it out.

The car came to a screeching halt. The driver door opened. A tall Negro man hopped out. It was Wendell.

They sent him to be the bearer of bad news. I knew it. I'd rather hear any news, good or bad, than nothing. My heart dropped as I ran over to him. His normally cool voice was full of emotion.

"We got a call and I think we got a lead."

17

Chapter 17

I ran to Carla and tossed Muddy's leash to her. She looked ready to faint. I told her I'd be back and flung the heavy passenger door open. He was there and gone in about fifteen seconds. Wendell managed to get that Ford Falcon from zero to sixty in about four seconds.

He whipped the winding corners like Speed Racer. This old man, never in a hurry, now had a fire lit under him. This had to be serious. I held onto the door handle as he bent the corners.

"What happened?" I asked him. My breath was short and my words ran together.

"We got a call down at the precinct with a tip of a man going inside a house with a young boy one day, and a little girl the next."

"How long ago was this?"

"About thirty minutes ago. Mitchells sent me right out to grab you. He wanted you to be there when we nab this motherfucker."

"I mean, w..where is this house?"

"Mitchells didn't say. He just told me to grab you."

I stared at him.

"What else did he say?"

"He didn't say much. But everyone is at the precinct gearing up."

The seat swallowed my body. I got the feeling that Wendell wasn't telling me the full story.

"Do they at least have a warrant?" I asked. He responded in robotic fashion.

"Mitchells is taking care of everything right now."

I stared out the window and tapped my foot as if I were driving. My mind raced with thoughts of who, and why.

We got back to the parking lot and he pulled up next to my car. I jumped in and realized I had been blocked in. I hopped the curb and left tire marks in the open field until I got back onto the asphalt. The two of us raced through the freeway towards downtown.

Once we got back to the precinct, I banged the door open with my shoulder. One of the secretaries almost received three weeks of injury leave. It just missed her face. When I got to the briefing room, I stood panting in the back. Mitchells looked proud and strong at the front. As officers, we lived for moments like this. Especially when it was for one of our own. Everyone turned to me and I nodded. Then he began his briefing.

He gave a rundown of things we were all too familiar with. The ages, names and all that. He pulled up photos of the kids on a large projector. My eyes stayed fixed on Tasha's smiling face. He replaced her photo with one of the suspect. It was Cyclops. Rage took over my body. I had just been there the night before. I knew why Wendell didn't tell me sooner. He knew I would've headed right over there by myself.

The world had been moving at eighty miles an hour since the

night before. My heart had constantly felt like it would explode. Then things had begun slowed down. I caught my breath. I could think again. Tasha had to be alive. If she wasn't, I'd kill every pusher within a fifty-mile radius.

Mitchells boasted how these crimes rarely happen in the city. He then pulled up another picture. Cyclops' hideous face stared at me. I studied every minute detail about him. The small cut on his eyebrow. The fragments of a beard that wouldn't connect. How his left ear was smaller than his right.

The call was made to the Eleventh Precinct who would run the raid with us. It turned out that there was a case being built against the twenty nine year old Cyclops who had troubles with the law before. Once in '66 for disturbing the peace at a near riot on Kercheval Street. He was dead set on being in a riot because he had been picked up the next year during the actual riots. He was considered armed and dangerous.

Three teams would operate the raid. Team Alpha would come through the alley to the back of the house. Team Bravo would breach the side door. Team Charlie would kick in the front door and take control of the situation.

He spoke on what to do if they encountered women and children in the house before dismissing the room. I went deaf. I'd kick anyone in the ribs if I had to. If anyone in that house had info, I'd get it out of them. Cyclops ceased to be a human to me.

I fiddled around with the bullet proof vest in the passenger seat. They always made me feel uncomfortable. Mitchells and I led a caravan of officers. We appeared to roll in slow motion, looking like an ominous funeral procession.

This was nothing new to the residents. Every other week some officers kicked in a dope spot. It was nothing to see young males laid out on the grass. Arms stretched out with shotguns to their heads. People walking down the street causally pointed at us. They probably placed bets on who we would hunt down today.

Mitchells had been speaking to me. I don't know about what and I don't know why. My mind was fixed on Tasha and Cyclops and I didn't give a damn what he had to say.

The caravan split up when we got close to the neighborhood. Mitchells parked along the side street. We had a direct view of the house. To our right was the Detroit Airport. There was a broken fence. Clearly one of the racers lost control of his vehicle the night before.

The teams exited their cars. Like trained assassins they slipped into their positions. It was quiet around there. Almost too quiet. Had someone tipped him off? Alpha team slipped into the alley to cut off escape routes. They stood by motionless and waited for the signal.

Tasha was inside waiting on me. I was five hundred feet away from who needed me most. I bounced my leg and nearly rocked the car. I unbuckled my seat belt and reached for the door.

Mitchells scolded me. As he was doing so, Officer Keith Flannigan strolled up the walkway. Keith was as Irish as they come. Those were his words, not mine. A spitting image of Mike from All in the Family. Mustache and all. His daddy's daddy had been a cop. It was all he knew.

Six officers all crouched behind the huge bushes that he passed. They calmly awaited his signal. Cool and collected, Keith knocked on the door and waited. The front door opened and boom.

A loud pop echoed from the backyard. A woman stood in a tank top at the front door. Keith flung open the screen and tossed her to the ground. All six officers behind him moved like worker ants carrying shotguns and entered the home. Mitchells and I both had our hands on the door knobs. The screams from inside would horrify anyone. They were quite normal to Mitchells and I.

After about a minute, we exited the car. Pistols in hand, we strolled towards the front door. As much as Mitchells pissed me off, our military backgrounds tethered us. We instinctively surveyed the area for threats.

Neither of us said a word, nor did we need to. He went around the driveway to the back of the house while I charged the front door.

With my pistol drawn, I tossed the door open. Cyclops and the woman were on their stomachs with their hands cuffed behind them. Cyclops cursed and screamed until Keith put his size twelves into his ribs. To my right was a couch. I pulled it away from the wall. The woman who opened the door grunted when I hit her with it. I pushed it back and stood over her.

"Is this his girl?" I asked.

"A fox like that ain't his mama," Keith said.

Cyclops raised his head over his shoulder. His good eye got a look at me.

"I should've known you punk motherfucker. I told you I ain't have nothing to do with that shit. Check the whole fucking house. Ain't no-"

He went on and on. As I walked towards him, my mind raced. I placed my shoe on his shoulder and gave him a good push. He came to rest on his back. I knelt down and looked into his eye.

"Where are they?"

"Man fuck you Jack. I ain't touch no fucking kids."

I swiped a shotgun from one of the officers. I aimed it straight at Cyclops' head. The whole city could hear the woman scream.

"Where are they?"

"Nigga you ain't gone shoot me. I'm already in handcuffs."

He was right. I couldn't shoot him. But I had never wanted to shoot someone so bad in my life. He knew where Tasha was. I was stuck. I looked over at Keith.

"Keith, we fired on him after he fired on us first right?"

"That's what I saw, Dom."

"Last chance," I said to Cyclops.

"You dirty fucking pigs."

Another officer emerged from the back of the house. He carried a crying child that was no older than two. I contained myself. The girl's mother screamed and wriggled to get free.

"Get your hands off of her," she said, nearly foaming at the mouth.

I returned the shotgun and held my hands out to the little girl. The officer handed her to me. She screamed even louder than her mother. I raised the horrified child up and down and bounced her in my arms.

Cyclops explained in great detail what he would do to me if I harmed her. I knelt down to him again with his daughter when a young officer named Charles came from the kitchen.

"There ain't no kids here Detective, but we did find something," he said.

He raised her up and down. The child was horrified. Fear knows no language. A young brother named Charles came from the kitchen.

"There ain't any kids here Detective, but we did find something."

I shimmied through the kitchen. Down the narrow steps. I ducked my head once in the basement. Bags of clothes were everywhere. I kicked them over.

The basement had a little bar area. On the bar were three revolvers and a rifle. Small tan bags of dope sat next to them. Well he wasn't Eddie Jackson or Frank Lucas but we had enough to book him. I tossed everything around looking for the kids. Garden equipment, charcoal, laundry hampers. Nothing.

I ran back up the steps and performed the same check around the house. It didn't take long. It was a modest house. I didn't find anything out of the ordinary. Nothing that even suggested he had other children in the house. I ran out back and found Mitchells standing over a dead pit bull.

"Did you check the garage?" I asked him.

The garage door opened from the inside. It was as clear as the day they brought the house. I stared at the dog. Mitchells said it started to growl so they shot it. The shooter, a white boy named Crowley tipped his hat.

I told Mitchells about the guns and drugs and went back to the side door. Cyclops was still on the ground giving Keith an earful. Keith gave it right back to him. I knelt by his head again.

"I'll ask you this one more time. Where-"

"Nigga are you deaf and dumb? I don't have shit and don't know shit," he said.

"And what about the guns and dope downstairs?"

"Man y'all planted that shit. This whole thing is a set up. You ain't got shit on me."

I stood up and looked at Keith.

"Throw him in the car, he's coming with us."

18

Chapter 18

We flung him in the back of Keith's squad car. Cyclops, Keith and I all flew down the Interstate towards downtown. Once we exited the freeway and got onto the streets, pedestrians stopped and watched us. When I wasn't going off on Cyclops, Keith was. We had good reason. He had a mouth on him and we nearly pulled into an alley to shut him up.

I remembered the days when we would actually find some VC soldiers. We'd display them like trophies in this almost inhumane way. It was a "look what I caught" type of thing. I hate to say it but that's just what it was. That always stated in my mind as I brought in suspects.

We pulled into the parking lot of the precinct and pulled him out the back. The gray clouds blocked the sun and brought a chill over the city. Cyclops had been screaming about being cold as I yanked him through the parking lot. I beamed with pride as I showed off my capture through the halls of the building.

It was time for one of the best parts of the job. I got to sit at a table across from grown men and watch them break down. Out of ten men, only two would hold up in an interrogation. Three would put up a fight but give in. The other five would break before you gave them a coffee. I got a feeling he would put up a decent fight.

I shoved him into the interrogation room and left Keith to guard him and get further acquainted.

The office had never seemed so quiet. I felt eyes on my every move. I grabbed a notepad off my desk and went into the break room. I reached for the coffee pot and it began to tremble. Hot coffee ran down my hand. I inhaled deeply and closed my eyes.

I felt more eyes on me. It was Chelle. She stood at the door, too afraid to speak. Right on cue, Mitchells walked in.

"I want to try something, Broddie."

"Try what?" I said. I looked up at him. What bullshit was he ready to pull?

"I'm going to let Detective Wright interrogate him."

The coffee cup slipped out of my hand. The unexpected clang made even me jump.

"What? No way. This is my case Lieutenant."

He didn't want me to be in charge of the room. He didn't trust me keeping my cool. It was always something with him. I put up a big fight. This was my daughter that I was looking for. I was the one up at night wondering where she was.

The two of us went back and forth for a few minutes. I was seconds away from telling him to shove his order up his ass. He lowered his head.

"Not another word, Broddie. That's my decision and that's how it's gonna be. It's the best option for finding these kids. That's final."

He turned and walked from me. Wendell walked right in after him.

"Look, Dom, this uh, it wasn't my idea. Mitchells, he uh–"

"I know it wasn't you, Dell. It was that fat motherfucker trying to cut me down man."

"We'll get answers out of him. Don't worry."

I try to never doubt another brother's competence. If it had been anyone else I would have raised hell. But I trusted Wendell. All the rumors said that he had once been a pretty good cop. A rough one, but a good one. Strangely, all the talk stopped there. Something turned him into the shell of a man that he was then. That was never explained.

We all had a basket on our desks where we kept our open cases. His had to have been two feet high. But Wendell was on the Force even before integration. That had to mean something right? They wouldn't let a mediocre Negro be a cop, especially for over twenty years. I knew that I'd have my answer soon.

Most criminals are masterminds of human psychology. They just don't know it. I assumed Cyclops was no different. I replaced my anger with a cool face of nonchalance. I glided into the room. I refused to let the built up rage slip. He would pick up on it and use it against me without a doubt.

Our interrogation room was nothing special. It was little more than a closet really. Small, cold, probably ten by eight feet. It had no windows and no clock. Time seemed to move real slow in there. I relieved Keith and set my coffee and notepad on the table and stared into his open eye.

"I think your buddy broke one of my ribs," he said.

"You're lucky that's all he broke. I'd do more."

He smiled.

"Oh you're a good little boy. You doing a great job showing out for 'massa'. A good little house nigger. Whipping around the bad ones showing massa you ain't like us. You're a fucking disgrace."

I held my cool. He almost got the reaction he wanted. He was good. Then again, I was on edge. A nun could have pissed me off.

The room was insulated to keep the noise out. He stopped talking and I could hear the ringing in my ear. We entered a stare down until the door opened. Wendell carried a cup of coffee in his mouth, another in one hand and two donuts in the other. He slid a coffee and one donut over to Cyclops. He eyed them as if they were poison.

"You think I'm gonna eat or drink that?" he said.

"It's there if you want it," Wendell said. His tone suggested he didn't care whether Cyclops took it or not. It was almost as if he wasn't actually speaking to Cyclops. More like he spoke out loud and Cyclops just happened to answer.

"You eat it first."

"No, I'm diabetic. Can I get you to stand up for me please?"

There were three chairs in the room. I stood in the corner near one with two being at the table. Cyclops had his back to the door. Wendell made him move closer to the wall.

Later he explained the psychology of it. That let Cyclops know that the way out of this room, was through him. Wendell snapped his fingers and exited the room again.

We entered another stare down. Both looking for signs of weakness. Sweat poured out of my underarms and from my hands. I stood there with the man who could tell me where my daughter was. The handcuffs jingled as he broke off a piece of the donut.

We were there to find my daughter and he was eating a snack. My face remained unchanged as I came towards him. He continued to chew. I don't know what I planned on doing until he opened his mouth.

"This is some good shit," he said.

I couldn't take it anymore. I grabbed him by the throat and squeezed as tight as I could. His cuffed hands pounded against my stomach. The chair leaned on two legs. He kicked the table back and made loud choking noises. My grip was tight and firm. I leaned down.

"Spit it out."

He ejected the chewed up donut on his lap and fell to the freezing floor. He gasped for air. His rough cough sounded someone starting up an old Model T. If he didn't hate me before, he did after that. We were going to throw down right there had Wendell not walked back in. He looked at Cyclops and turned to me. Disappointment was all over his face as he helped Cyclops back to his chair, apologizing the entire time.

"That's not how we do things," he continued to say.

"Take these cuffs off me and let's see you do that," Cyclops said to me.

"Woah, they'll be none of that," said Wendell. "We're going to do this the right way, you got that, Broddie?"

I managed a grunt. It was enough compliance for us to continue. Wendell slid the other donut over to Cyclops who gave it a one eyed glare. He also set a cover on the table.

"I brought you this, I know it can be a little cold in here. It even makes me uncomfortable."

Cyclops stayed silent.

"As you see, there's your coffee and a new donut. I don't know if you got the chance to eat or not. I know when I don't eat, I get really cranky and don't want to talk. I hope I have enough cream and sugars in there. If not, I can always go get you another. How about a water for your throat? It's no biggie."

Silence.

"Well my name is Detective Wendell Wright. I've been with the Detroit Police going on twenty-four years. I was a street cop who ran around doing some pretty bad things to the residents. Right after the riots, I was given a desk gig to 'teach me' but it really was to save my life."

After he said the word "riots", there was a change in Cyclops. He appeared uncomfortable. I stood in the corner with my arms folded and studied his every move.

"I'm not gonna lie. A lot of folks didn't like me. I was a "Tom" as you might say. But you'll find I'm pretty laid back now. I understand both sides of the law. I treat even suspected criminals with respect. You haven't been convicted yet, right? I'll give you the respect you deserve as will Detective Broddie or we'll have him dismissed."

More silence.

On the other hand, I nearly dropped my jaw. Old Man Wendell was one of the cops we complained about. One of the cops that started the riot. Or maybe he said it for shock value. It seemed honest enough though. He looked down at a folder in front of him.

"Alright, Cyrus Edwards. I see here that you're no stranger to the law. A felony breaking and entering. Ah, the most heinous is during the riots. Picked up for assault, battery and arson."

"A white boy burned that store," he said. Then he sealed his lips again.

"I'm sure. Well Cy, can I call you Cy? Don't be shy here. I'm very relaxed compared to my coworkers. This isn't my first rodeo so if you have any questions, feel free to stop me. Are you hungry at all? I can get you a good meal. Pancakes, sausage, eggs, all the good stuff."

I was to learn later that this technique was common. The

key was to keep the suspects mind racing. Never give them a minute to stop and think.

Cyclops was silent. Wendell began the method he had practiced for twenty-four years. He bombarded Cyclops with details and bullshit information. From the time he first got on the force, to his favorite partner.

He lectured on the racist policies. How our coworkers wanted to lock Cyclops up regardless of if he did it or not. After about twenty minutes, Cyclops' armor began to crack. He folded his arms and began bouncing his leg. It was brutal to sit through. I wondered how many men had fallen to it.

After about minute thirty five I began to grow restless as well. Under normal situations I could do this all day. But with the weight of Tasha's disappearance, I shifted my body in the corner. Wendell still asked questions and droned on. Finally, Cyclops broke. He sat up.

"Look, I ain't do shit. I don't have shit. And I don't know shit about what you're talking about."

Wendell held his smile in.

"Cy, I know you've seen the news. You know why you're here. We don't want you here all night. My wife is making meatloaf tonight. I want to go get in that. But I need to know why I keep hearing your name. Especially when it comes to some missing kids. It doesn't look good for you buddy."

Cyclops continually professed his innocence. Even to the guns and dope. Wendell questioned it. These two were like something off a bad TV show. My arms were wrapped tight around my body. I nearly cut off my circulation.

My plan had been to not speak anymore unless spoken to. But the more I sat there and listened, the harder that became. Again, I snapped.

"Look you piece of shit, you got two fucking minutes to tell me where my daughter is or there ain't a cop in this city that will be able to pull me off you."

Oh he called me every name in the book. Cyclops was guilty. He had to be. All signs pointed to him. But then why did I believe him when he said he "would never do no sick shit like that". Wendell tried to pull back some order in the room.

"You know what I think Cy?"

"That he's a bitch?" Cyclops said referring to me.

"No. I think dope is a big business. We've seen guys go from dirt broke to make thousands of dollars a day. Maybe the Reverend pissed you off. He comes in all high and mighty and tries to stop all that bread you're bringing in."

"I never touched dope a day in my life."

"We see it all the time Cy. You had to get him off your back. He kept pushing so you send him a little message. I think that boy is safe right now. Shaken up, but safe."

There was no change in Cyclops' expression this time.

"Then Detective Broddie comes sniffing around and pisses you off again. Another sell-out cop. A brother who works for the Man. You need to send him a message as well. But you never counted on the neighborhood selling you out. Am I at least close Cy?"

Silence.

"Look, I need something Cy. When I walk out that door, the next person to come in won't help you. It will only get worse from here. You know it, and I know it."

"I told y'all, I don't know shit about no little girl."

"Then where were you two days ago at around four o'clock."

He gave us a detailed description of his day. Pointless activities mostly. Then he got to the meat of it.

"At three o'clock I picked my oldest daughter Laura up from Nolan Elementary. Call and ask them. Then I take her to get some McDonald's and straight to her grandma's house while I go home and do what I gotta do."

"And what do you gotta do, Cy?"

"What I need to."

"Like snatching children?"

"I just told you to check my fucking alibi. How could I grab some kid if I'm grabbing my own daughter at the same time?"

"And what time did you say you picked her up?"

"Around three o'clock."

"Dom, did you hear four, cause I thought he said two thirty?"

I finally decided to sit down. Directly across the table, I stared at him.

"Dell, I heard much earlier, like around one forty."

"Man fuck y'all, I said three o'clock. Same time every day."

"And what about the next day?" Wendell asked.

"I just said same time every day. Check my alibi. You ain't got shit on me and you wasting your time. You ain't find not one trace of them kids in my house."

"What if we searched your mother's house? Tina Edwards? Here it says she was picked up for assaulting an officer back in '58? We're noticing a pattern."

"You ain't gone find shit there either."

"Look, Cy, you seem like a good kid, I wanna help you. I hate seeing young brothers locked up. You are being looked at for two things now. One happens to be the guns and narcotics that we found in your house. That's indisputable, Cy. The other happens to be the missing children. Let me remind you that we got a call straight to your house. You can either tell us where the children are and you go to jail for that, or you can act like you don't know anything and go to prison for both."

Silence.

"You haven't touched your donut Cy, go ahead, it's glazed."

"I'll do one hundred years under the jail for drugs and guns before I ever admit to some shit about kids that I didn't do. Do what the fuck you gotta do."

Just then the door was thrust open. A short balding man in a big suit pointed at Cyclops. Good old Curtis Abelman. The guy thought he was a big shot. He had cost us more than one conviction over the years.

"Shut up. Whatever you are thinking about saying, shut up." He turned his attention to us. "Detectives Wright and Broddie, bending the law as usual. Back to your old tricks huh Wendell?"

"Bending the law?" Wendell said.

"Come on, Cyrus, you're coming with me."

"Like hell he is."

"You have absolutely zero evidence that my client has those children. Cyrus, where were you when they allege you abducted the children?"

"Like I told them, picking up my daughter from school, Nolan Elementary and dropping her off at her grandma's house."

"You heard the man. You can get the school on the phone right now and they will repeat verbatim what he just said. Not only that, there is the issue of this."

He slammed a piece of paper on the desk.

"What is this gentlemen?"

I looked at the warrant and stated the obvious. Abelman spoke again.

"It is the warrant. And is the written purpose of said warrant?"

"For the search and seizure of narcotics, narcotics paraphernalia and weapons."

"If your warrant is for seizing drugs and weapons, why are you tossing things around my client's home looking for children?"

Wendell stepped in.

"Look slick, we received an anonymous phone call saying that he was seen with the children."

"Then your warrant needs to be for the search of the missing children. We have laws for a reason detectives. You all can't be this incompetent. You have illegally searched my client's home and brought him in on unverified charges."

"Well, we still have him on the drug charges which the warrant was issued for."

"See this? What is this?" the lawyer pointed.

"That's the date of issue."

"As you know, or I hope you know, warrants must be executed within 56 days of their ordering. Now I wasn't a math major at U of D Mercy but I believe this date was 72 days ago which make it null and void. Let's go son, you're going home."

Cyrus stood up and smirked at us. He grabbed the donut and took a huge bite out of it.

"Come on, come on, don't antagonize them. You gentlemen will be hearing from us again for a violation of his constitutional rights."

And just like that, my main suspect was gone. We had him and he slipped through our hands. He had an alibi, true. But we had him on the drug charges. Those assholes at the Eleventh Precinct fucked it all up. Who the fuck just sits on a warrant like that? I flipped the table up against the wall and felt water stream down my face.

"Fuck," I screamed. How was I going to tell Carla that my

only lead slipped through my fingers like that? Wendell looked over at me.

"I'm frustrated too Dom, I thought we had something but don't worry, we're going in the right direction."

19

Chapter 19

Back to square one. I stood in the center of that cold room with Wendell's hand on my shoulder. He didn't know what to say any more than I. I turned my head towards him. Were his eyes always that far apart? And why were they moving even further from each other?

The walls felt like they were closing in on me. Wendell's face began to grow and distort like he was a fun house mirror. I staggered to the door and made a straight line to the front door. Down the steps, I bounced from wall to wall like a pin ball.

I did my best to pull it together and appear normal. Officer Isaac spoke and waved at me. I couldn't make sense of his words though. I finally reached outside. I took a deep breath, hoping that the open air would help.

I needed to get out of there. Just for a minute. I hopped in my car and pulled off. I nearly flattened a brother on the way out the driveway. By the time he picked up a rock to throw, I was already on the Lodge Freeway heading north. I left the car on autopilot. It zipped through and around traffic. A gold sedan nearly lost its mirrors. The fool tried to switch lanes before I shot the gap.

I turned the radio up to full blast. Sonny Eliot was giving the weather. I needed music but every station was on commercial. It only added to my frustration so I switched it off.

Before I knew it, I had passed Wyoming Street. The retaining walls started to close in on me. But it wasn't just the freeway, the car itself sucked me in. I had about three miles to go before the walls ended. I wheezed and struggled to catch my breath. This made me panic even more.

I tossed the steering wheel to the right. I nearly took out a semi-truck as I slammed on the brakes. I kicked up dust and smoke in the narrow shoulder of the freeway. The car came to rest within six inches of hitting the towering, thirty foot tall, concrete retaining wall. I grabbed my pocket knife and cut the seat belt off me. I pushed open the door and jumped out onto the freeway.

A mustang swerved and blasted its horn at me. It had to be going sixty miles an hour. I staggered back to the car and leaned on the trunk. I don't know how long I was there but a car pulled up behind me. It might have been a Chevelle, I can't recall.

The door opened and a woman came out. She was absolutely gorgeous. Even better than Thelma. But it wasn't in a sexual light. She was more graceful than anything. She appeared to float towards me. Her huge Afro bounced. The sun kissed her dark skin.

"Woah brother, that was wild. I saw you swerving. Are you good?"

I struggled to maintain my breath. I watched her and her car for a moment. I finally got a hold of myself. I had just woken up from a bad dream. The cars roared by us at seventy miles an hour.

"Uh, yeah, yeah, I'm fine. Just a little stressed."

I wonder if she could see through my armor.

She handed me a bottle of water. Apparently, I looked a little pale. Drinking after someone went against my rules. Especially a random stranger. But in that moment, I'd sip off the straw of a dope fiend. I downed the bottle and turned it upside down. When every drop was gone I searched for my wallet.

"I'm sorry," I said. "I don't have any bread on me. Let me get your phone number and I can bring you the cash."

"Don't worry about it brother. It's just a little water. I'm sure they will make more," she smiled.

"Thank you so much sister, I really appreciate it."

"Don't mention it. But be cool, don't let these white folks break you down. Stay strong. Peace."

Those simple words refilled me. She hopped back in her car and waited for a clear spot to pull off. Then she was gone.

Sam Cooke sang about how Jesus gave him water. I ain't one of them superstitious Negroes. I pay attention to my left-hand itching. Walking under ladders. Breaking a looking glass and all that shit. But I even wondered if she actually existed or not.

I stood under the exit sign for Seven Mile Rd. I realized I must have been headed for my parents' house. That had been my place of guidance for thirty years. I knew they'd be at my house with Carla. I merged back onto the freeway and headed a course for home.

I stood on the porch motionless for a second. They heard me pull up. They had to be waiting in anxiety for news. What would I tell them? How would I tell them? I hated feeling like that. Jittery and nervous.

I fiddled with the keys and pushed open the door. Carla sat in her mother's arms. She stood up and ran to me. She begged me to speak. I surveyed the room. All their eyes were full of foolish hope. For hours, they felt that I would walk in with Tasha. It hurt to have to be the one to take their dreams away.

"We had a lead," I said. They rose up. "But it turned out to be bullshit." All the air left the room. They dropped their heads. Even Pops, which shocked me. Let him tell it, he had no emotions to show. He sat at the dining room table next to mom. I walked passed everyone and went to the back. I nodded my head at him on the way. He knew what that meant.

I made a detour to the kitchen and grabbed a beer. Pop followed me through the den. We passed Tasha's untouched toys. The piano that Carla tried to force her to play. I could hear her butchering "Twinkle Twinkle Little Star" in my mind. Pop and I went out back and stood on the porch overlooking what used to be my garden.

Our breaths swirled away from us as we spoke. When I was young I thought I'd have all the answers by the time I was thirty. I was a grown man. Paid bills. Had an overpriced mortgage. I even had my own family and was responsible for teaching my own child how to live, but I still felt lost. I always felt like a child again when I went to my Pop. I don't know if all men felt like that. Maybe we do, but we just don't talk about it.

Pop was the typical old school father. He wouldn't be caught dead saying he loved you. That was for sissies. But you knew he did love you deep down. Like I said before, we had never hugged. But I knew he wanted to. Dads like him had too much other stuff going on back then. Fighting some white pecker woods at the job. Finding a place to live. Men were different then. They were too busy providing and protecting to care about that shit.

I told him the details of the case and our ordeal with Cyclops. Pops was a practical man. Two plus two made four. He would never consider one times four made four also.

"Why would someone call in a tip on an innocent man?" he asked.

"Maybe somebody doesn't like him. They were fu-I mean playing games with us to get to him. Or maybe he isn't as innocent as he seems."

"Which do you think it is?"

I rubbed my beard stubble.

"I hate to say it, but I think he's innocent. I just, I don't have nowhere else to turn. I mean there's another potential suspect that I pissed off but he ain't take Tasha."

"Who is that?"

"Some little wanna be Panther that gave us some trouble. I made him into an informant for me."

"Maybe he called on the pusher."

I pondered. Pop spoke.

"It sounds like if you could find out who made that call, you'd be able to put all the pieces together."

"That's what I was thinking. But who? And why? If somebody was gonna dime on him for dope, they would've been done it by now. It just don't make no sense."

"To be honest, that sounds like something a white boy would do."

"What?"

I turned from my dying tomatoes and stared at him.

"To call the police on an innocent brother? Well he ain't innocent cause he's a pusher. But that's what them white folks do all the time. Just to fuck with us."

"Yeah, it does, doesn't it?"

"Your mama had the news on last night and they were talking about some child killer up in Oakland County. They think it's a white boy. I'm not saying it could be the same guy but that's a crime that brothers don't do."

I never thought about it. There was a reason I always came to the old man. I needed to find whoever made that call. Even if they knew nothing about the case, it was the only lead I had. I had to exhaust it.

I ran through my memories. I had spoken to some white cat just hours earlier. I couldn't remember his name. I barely remembered his face. I had so much on my mind these past few days.

"I gotta go call the Reverend," I said.

"I think that's your best bet. But there's something else more important right now."

"What's that?"

"Get in there and hug your fucking wife."

The words hit like a brick. Pop never intervened in my marriage. Even when I would ask him questions, he usually let me figure things out for myself. For him to bring it up meant something. I gave him a blank stare.

"Huh? What do you mean?'

"You been leaving her alone through all this shit. She's the main one you need to be around right now."

"But I ain't left her alone. She got y'all and–"

"She needs you," he interrupted. "She don't need us."

"But–"

"God damn it, but nothing. You ain't learn nothing from watching my mistakes? By protecting and loving Tasha, you have to do the same for her mama as well. I ain't gonna mention it again, it's your marriage. She–"

The back door burst open. Carla was frantic and ran on just on cue.

"Dom, come to the phone. It's Chelle from your office."

Chelle? It was Saturday, so why was she still at the office? I ran inside and up the steps to the dining room.

"Hello?"

"Dom, two things. One, some guy called to talk to you."

"What'd he say?"

"He said the car you're looking for was an old beat up Chevy."

"I need to come to the office for that?"

"Well no, not for that but there's also a woman here that claims to have some information for you."

I threw the phone back on the wall hook. I ran towards the door when I remembered what Pop told me. I stopped and turned around. All eyes were on me.

I went to Carla and wrapped my arms around her and whispered in her ear. I recited one of the letters I had wrote her while in Vietnam. I told her how the thought of her kept me going. It took a lot for me to even say those things to her. But after they were out, I felt lighter. It was strange.

I told the room what Chelle said and that I'd be back. I ran out the front door and hopped back into my car. The Reverend would have to wait. I needed to see who this was at the office.

20

Chapter 20

The drive back to the office was a blur. I guess that says a lot about where my mind was. I ran up to the third floor. When I burst through the doors, Chelle was waiting on me. I knocked the doors open. Chelle stared right at me. Her wishful eyes put me at ease. She stood up and came around her desk and directed me to my left. I hadn't notice but a woman was sitting ten feet from me.

"Hello again," she said while sitting cross legged.

I remembered that voice.

"Mrs. T-I mean, Ms. Turner, how are you?"

"I'm well." Her answer was short. Her arms were folded tight across her.

"If this is about the murdered officer I'll give my partner a call and he'll-" I said before she cut me off.

"It's not about that. It's about Cyrus."

"Yes, yes, please follow me to the interview room."

One word was the main difference between our interview room and our interrogation room. Interview just sounded nicer. It put the person at ease.

On our way to the room, we passed Wendell and Walters. I led her to her seat and excused myself. I grabbed Wendell to help me take notes. He gladly accepted. We entered the room together and took our seats. He sat to my left with Vaughn on my right.

I got the formalities out of the way and got right to the subject at hand.

"What do you have to tell us about Cyrus?"

"You ran up in the wrong guy's house."

"Yes, we know that now. Is that what you want–"

"No, there's more. I attend Reverend Brown's church. Him and Cyrus ran into a little problem some time back. One of the Reverend's sidekicks got into it with him. They were going around trying to clean up the neighborhood."

"Yes, I've heard about this. What are you getting at?"

"It's the cat he got into it with that don't sit right with me."

She sat up straight and rested on her elbows and continued.

"He's far out man. A real weird cat. If I didn't see him in church, he's the type that I would avoid. He gives me the creeps. His name is Steven Wheeler. Write that down."

This was the man that I had met earlier. I let her continue.

"Cyrus has always been a hot head. Him and that white boy got into it and Cyrus threatened to shoot him. Word on the vine is that it was real bad. Steven even pissed on himself. Later that day they said he was swinging at the air in tears and shit, saying he would get Cyrus back for that."

"How do you know that about Cyrus?"

"Because that's my nephew that you were kicking around."

I tried a look of concern. I didn't want to make it too obvious that I didn't give a crap.

"So, you think Steven called in a false report to get back at

Cyrus?"

"You might think it sounds strange but it's as right as rain to me. Now I ain't saying that it's definitely him but who else would it be?"

I was able to look pass the anger she now had for me. Her eyes seemed sincere enough. She kept talking.

"That ain't all though. He's had a problem or two with the Reverend."

"And what are those?"

"I do know that he gets in trouble with some of the women around the church."

"Some of the women?" I asked.

"He always trying to get him some chocolate. He pushed up on me a while back. We all just kind of tolerate him. But he's a space cadet. I try to be nice and churchly to everyone but he takes it too far."

She pulled a cigarette out of her purse and lit it.

"The son of a bitch took that as his chance to ask me out. He'd walk me to my car. Buy me little bullshit and even tried to follow me home one day. I had to tell the Reverend to do something about it or I'd tell my nephew."

"What did the Reverend do?"

"I guess he talked to him. He just told me that he would handle it. Steven backed off after that. Actually, he disappeared for like a month and then came back. That motherfucker ain't never sat right with me. He's the type that would do some shit like call in a fake report."

"You sure you aren't just making sure your nephew gets off the hook?"

"Look, if he was guilty, he'd still be in here wouldn't he? That boy ain't take no kids. Does he do some stupid shit? Of course. But his mama would beat his ass if he even thought about harming some kid. Hell, I'd beat his ass."

She stopped and took a puff and blew.

"I ain't have no reason to suspect Steven of anything except being a man. All men are creeps. But I went to college and ain't nobody's dummy. All of what I told you just now, lets me know that some shit in the water ain't clean. And Steven is stirring it good."

"Does he live around here?"

"Oh no. I heard him say one time that he had a thirty minute drive to church one Sunday. He stays far."

"Do you know what he drives?"

"He drives this beat up, blue Plymouth."

"What year?"

"Ah hell, I don't know that."

"How about a description of Steven?"

I couldn't remember much about him. Other than his wild hair and him being white. Even though he stood out like a sore thumb, he just flew under the radar. Her descriptions jogged my memory. Huge glasses usually sat on his thin nose. He was perhaps in his early or mid-thirties. About six feet tall and real skinny like a high school boy. He walked with a strange bounce in his step.

"Have you told the Reverend any of this?" I asked.

"No. Something told me to check on my nephew today. I'm glad I did."

She cut her eyes at me. If what she was saying had any merit, I'd feel bad. But not until I found out. She could be jiving too. I thanked her and told her I would go visit the Reverend Brown and Steven right away.

She didn't look at me as I led her out. No goodbye or nothing.

That Steven son of a bitch knew something. I could feel it. He had been right under my nose. If I could get to him, I could make all of this make sense. I began to sweat. What if it were too late? I prayed for those Tasha and Junior to be safe. I called out to Wendell.

"Hey Dell, can you do me a solid?"

"What's that?" he asked.

"Put out an APB for this guy. I'm going to visit the Reverend."

21

Chapter 21

The Davison Freeway was just as slick as it looked. A light drizzle turned into sporadic downpours. It's a wonder how I didn't hydroplane and spin out into the concrete barrier that divided the two sides. I grit my teeth and vice gripped the steering wheel as I weaved in and out of traffic, terrorizing motorists.

The rain brought some much needed tranquility to the area. Other than the rain or an occasional car driving by, I sat outside the Reverend's church in silence. I reached to take the keys out of the ignition when a figure at the back of the church caught my eye.

It held an umbrella and shifted through the dumpster. Unnatural looking and hunched over, it looked more beast than man. I pulled the car to a slow creep and rolled down my window. It was about twenty feet from me.

It jumped when I gave the horn a light tap.

"This is a private residence brother," I said to it.

The Reverend turned towards me. I didn't think eyes could turn that color. The dark red in them indicated his fading health.

I couldn't hide my look of horror. I knew he wouldn't make it much longer in that condition. I needed to find the kids before I turned out the same.

It was like someone had shocked him with 100 volts. His short limbs seized up as he jumped at the sound of my voice. The fall from the top of the mountain shattered his spirit. I was all too familiar with the pathetic attempt at a smile went across his face. It indicated a broken man, and I had seen my fair share.

He reminded me of some of the villagers. Everything they owned and held dear went up in flames. With red eyes, they watched in terror as their homes turned into smoke signals. I yelled out to him.

"Reverend, what the hell are you doing out here?"

He paused for a moment and composed himself. The cold rain hit the sleeve of my jacket.

"Just some old food," he said. "It sat out too long. Wh..what are you doing here Detective?"

"Get in. It might really start coming down soon."

That was a big mistake. I should have made him walk. The aroma of a whiskey drinking, wet dog was then trapped in my car. I kept the window down. It was the only way to focus otherwise.

I made a U-turn and pulled in front of the church. His wife had been standing at the front door and vanished when she saw me. Her condition wasn't much better than his.

"Please tell me you have good news Detective?" he said.

"That's what I'm here to find out. Some just came to my office and told me some information."

"What was it?"

"She told me about Steven Wheeler. He was at the search this morning."

"Yes, he's also one of the ushers. What about him?"

"My informant told me some interesting things about him."

I gave him the run down on everything. His expression went from concern to anger.

"Now you wait just a minute," he said. "I've looked after that boy for years now. You're telling me you think he took my son?"

"No, I don't. But time is running out and anybody involved is a suspect. "

He exhaled and flooded the car with more of that putrid smell.

"Detective, it's as I feared. You-"

I didn't have the luxury of listening, so I cut in.

"You told me that you didn't have any enemies. Now I'm finding them all over. I'll ask you once and only once. Did you and Steven ever have any type of beef?"

"I..." He hesitated.

"Let me rephrase and be perfectly clear. Because now my daughter is involved. Would Steven have any reason to be angry at you? Is there a reason he would call on Cyclops?"

He slumped back in the seat and stared down at the door handle. A woman in a trench coat and heels walked by. She bent down and offered her services. I shooed her away. Then the Reverend spoke.

"Do you know that is was him who gave the tip?"

"No, it's a hunch."

"He and I have had our differences like any normal people, but nothing that would have him involved in something like this."

"And what are those differences?"

"He just showed up one day. All men are sinners and children of God so I don't discriminate on color. The parish family thought it was strange but we let him join and he became one of us. I felt honored that this white man would come to little me for help. We spent a lot of time together."

He pulled the seat up.

"That boy came up hard. You'd recognize his daddy before he did. Him and his sisters all got split up when they sent his mama to a looney house. Everything that ever meant anything was taken from him."

His speech continued. Mostly about how he had taken Steven in as somewhat of a son. His pace quickened as he became more defensive. The thought of Steven having anything to do with it sent him for a spin. Or maybe he just loved white folks. I rushed him to get to the point.

"A white boy wanting to be around Negroes all the time ain't odd to you?"

"It's not that simple with him. Because of how he grew up, he believes that Negro families are closer than white ones. He said that's why white families always hire a Negro to clean and watch the kids, it's just different. I guess when he's around us, he feels some sense of community, having turned his back on his own. Him and Junior were friends. Played ball together sometimes. I just don't see him having something to do with this."

I pulled my foot off the gas a bit. The way the conversation was going, he wouldn't give me anymore information if he thought it would be damning to Steven. If anything, he'd call him himself. I needed to lower his defenses.

'From what I gather," I started, "he don't sound like a bad cat at all. Maybe just misled and had a beef with the wrong cat. I gotta talk to him. At least to clear his name."

"Ain't much clearing necessary. He even works around kids. You can't work around kids when you're a danger right?"

"What does he do?"

"He works at this middle school. Maintenance work and sometimes serving the lunches."

"What's it called? And do you have his address?"

"Let me run to my office."

I rolled up my window and we both exited the car. I followed right behind him. When he stopped suddenly, I nearly ran him over.

"Actually Detective, my wife is inside with the girls. They're having a difficult time with their brother being gone. We don't want anyone in the building at the moment. I fear that the sight of you would give her another episode."

From the way she scampered away from the door, I believed him. I was running myself ragged looking for her son. I thought she would welcome my presence, but I didn't have time for petty battles. I hurried back to the car and waited.

Was he always this strange? This jittery and hunched over? Some men handled pressure and others cracked under it.

Was God happy with him? He was one of his strongest soldiers after all right? Sunday after Sunday, he told the world to stand strong. That when a giant came to fight, you stand strong and kill it with a slingshot. With God's help, men can be tossed into a furnace and walk out unharmed. Well, I had seen firsthand, how untrue that was. His congregation would have melted if they saw what Brown had become in the heat of fire.

I'd never tell my mother this. But I felt something watching this pious man beaten. This man who had judged me for acts of war. This man that stood on the mountain and pointed his finger at all the sinners, was now down among us. I wouldn't call it happiness. That ain't the word. But I felt something.

I must have sat there for ten minutes. I yanked the keys out of the ignition and opened the door. I jogged to the Church and opened the front door slow. The rush of alcohol violated me again. The Reverend stood face to face with me. I jumped back out into the sidewalk.

"Why are you coming to my door?" he asked.

"Look, I don't have time to-"

"No, I asked you nicely to stay in the car. Pam really doesn't want to see you."

I squinted my face.

"Are you alright Reverend?"

"Why, yes, yes, it's just been a long couple of days." He coughed.

"And you didn't call Steven while you were in there?"

"Of course not. Here's his phone number and address."

He had written them on an envelope. I snatched it from him and ran to the car. I thought I bled out all my pity in a jungle. But when I looked at him from the car, it overwhelmed me. His Godly armor was gone and he was helpless. Just like a regular old man. I yelled out to him.

"I'm just going to see what he knows. Please Reverend, go inside and get some rest. I'll come by after I see him."

"Okay thank you. Please, be gentle with Steven. The boy is very fragile."

"Do you need me to walk you upstairs?"

"No, no, I'll be fine."

He bumped into the front door as I pulled off. I flew north on Van Dyke with my mind racing just as fast as the car. Is this even the guy who called in the tip? Why would he have done it? I couldn't make sense of any of it. It had to be Cyclops. Who else would take Junior? Hopefully this Steven could tie some strings together.

Every day we duck and dodge things that can kill us. Bullets, car accidents. Those things were easy to avoid. You don't want to get shot? Move to a better neighborhood. You don't want a car accident? Drive slower. We can quantify those things.

But the fight against things we can't see is much worse. Stress, pain, regret and anger. They were all giving the Reverend fits. In just three days, he aged over five years. I was headed down that path. I couldn't become like that. I needed to be optimistic.

I would find those kids. As I zipped up the street, I truly believed it.

22

Chapter 22

It was a straight shot going north on Van Dyke. Crossing Eight Mile, I entered into hostile lands. The stares began immediately. Maybe they watched me because the car began to wobble and swerve into the median. I caught myself. My hands were shaking. Not just shaking, they were quaking. Another trait I thought I lost in the jungle. More of them seemed to have come back even harder.

What the hell about him made me afraid? I had been around him at least twice before so why did the thought of him make me feel uneasy? Would he really have something to do with two Negro children missing? The thought of a "yes" to that question sparked images of another riot.

I had never been that far up Van Dyke before. Shitty motels that weren't twenty years old, sat on every corner. Either those or some manufacturing plant. All the jobs that had once been in Detroit, crossed Eight Mile into places like this. It had been an open countryside just a few years before. There were new developments all around but the further out I went, the more of that flat, green land returned.

I pulled into a small subdivision. Back in Detroit there was a housing project called the Brewsters that opened in the 40s. Those towers had begun to become a cesspool for all things crime and desolation. Well, this subdivision made the Brewsters look like a Manhattan high rise. The general consensus is that the ghetto is for Negroes. Well I should've taken photos of this place. It could've made the cover of Time.

Children had played with their toys and dropped and tossed them all around the front yards. Trashcans were either kicked or blown over in the middle of the street. Maybe the raccoons had gotten to them the night before. Beat up pickup trucks sat in front of the trailers. The bottoms were eaten away by rust.

If the Waltons were from Michigan, they'd live there. The show's opening played in my mind. I could picture that old jalopy coming down the road. A bunch of barefoot white kids would run out to it.

Every time I crept passed a trailer, one row of blinds would be pulled down. After a few seconds, they would snap back. A man came out onto the little porch of one of the trailers. I felt more at home rolling through a Vietnamese village than there. He didn't need to tell me to get the hell out. I just knew.

The road continued to twist and turn and wind. I began to feel that I was going in circles. Some of the trailers had addresses. Some didn't. They all began to look the same to me. I felt trapped. Who would want to live like this? I thought.

It was like being in that jungle again. Surrounded on all sides. Don't know where to escape. I would have lost my cool had I not seen it. A blue trailer sat far back from the road on a nice plot of land. Pop would love it.

The trailer didn't have a paved driveway. Only a worn path that the tires had made over the years. The orange and red leaves surrounded the property on three sides. At the end of the path was a beat up, powder blue Plymouth Fury. I reached for my note pad. Just as Vaughn had described it.

It was just my look. Steven was home and I'd get answers out of him one way or another. I sat for a moment and took deep breaths to slow my heart rate. Nothing could stop me from shaking. I shut off the car and stayed still. I reached inside my jacket pocket and rubbed the six shot revolver. It gave me just enough comfort.

I opened my door slow to an eerie silence. It was peaceful out there. There was only the sound of rain drops hitting the tops of cars and trailers. Occasionally cars drove by some ways off. I closed the door as gently as I could and tip toed up the muddy path. I peered inside his car. Some old pop cans. A McDonald's bag.

I turned to his trailer and inched my way to it. Like feathers, my feet went up the steps unheard. The blinds were shut tight in the living room. A blue light from the TV peaked from the cracks. A studio audience laughed inside.

I knocked on the door. Well, actually I tapped on it with the joint of my middle finger. Then I did it twice. And then three times. I put my ear on the door and waited patiently.

Someone moved inside. I tapped on the door again. A couple seconds later, the same noise. It came from the far left of the trailer. The porch stopped before the window to that room. I stretched my neck to try to see into it. Of course, the blinds were closed. I jogged down the steps and went over to the window. It stood about three feet over my head.

I kept hearing that same noise. Was it her? My heart raced. I ran to the front door and was just shy of kicking it in when I heard a faint noise from behind the trailer. I froze for a few seconds and heard it again. I drew my revolver and went to investigate.

Peaking around the corner, I saw a camper big enough for maybe two people. It sat about a few hundred yards out. The hitch sat on cinder blocks. The beaten down door creaked as it opened.

A thin, slimy looking man emerged from the trailer. He carried a bucket in one hand and a fishing rod in the other. His hands and wrists were huge. I wondered if he was ex-military.

He walked over to a creek at the back of the property. His body looked twisted and unnatural. He whistled to himself. I waited until he turned his back to me to call out to him.

"Steven? Steven Wheeler?"

The dirt and grass under my feet made squishing sounds. I trampled the uncut mess. He stopped dead in his tracks and turned towards me. The way he did it, sent shivers down my spine.

"How can I help you?" He dropped the rod and bucket. Although his body tensed up, there was no emotion in his voice. He spoke low and ominous.

"You know why I'm here. You've seen me several times. I'm just here to ask you a couple questions."

I produced my badge and gave him my name and rank. Those things would usually lower a man's defenses.

"You're here without permission," he complained.

"Steven, I-"

"I don't want you here. So you have to leave. This is America... "

He went off on a tangent about our rights. He gave a colorful speech on how Fidel Castro would've promoted me for violating his property. The longer his lecture went, the more I determined that I would not leave. It was all so strange. Maybe Castro would give me a medal for it. But I was going to violate every last one of his rights if it meant it would lead to Tasha and Junior.

Reverend Brown said that Steven wanted a place to belong. He felt outcast his whole life. I decided to use some diplomacy in that instance. I gave him a false sense of camaraderie.

"Woah Steven, let's be cool brother. No one's trampling on your rights. Your name comes up and I just want to clear it. I gotta check on every lead, you dig?"

"Why would my name come up? I was leading one of the search parties for Junior," he screamed.

"I know, I know. I saw you. But I'm trying to figure out why I keep hearing your name. You told me about your problems with Cyclops but what about the Reverend?"

"I don't have to speak to you. You're trespassing on my property."

"This land is owned by the church Steven. I have permission to be here."

If he wasn't angry before, he sure was after that reveal. Steven was another beneficiary of brown's more, philanthropic side.

"But I live here. Reverend Wallace has always looked out for me. Why would I have any problems with him?"

"Well Steve, I know that isn't true. Can we step inside? I wanna get out of this rain. It's really starting to pick up and I can barely hear you from back there."

"No. I'm fine right here. I'm doing some fishing."

"You know they're more aggressive in the rain." I crossed my fingers after saying it. Luckily he latched on to the bait. Those defenses dropped nice and low for the moment.

"You fish?"

"Since I was old enough to walk. What bait you got going?"

We went back and forth about fish and nature for a few minutes. I got antsy but it was necessary. I tried to reel the conversation back in. He said something about respect for the "true God". I asked him what it meant. I don't even know if I was truly interested or just playing along.

"Apparently there are two Gods," he began. "One that lives in the fairy tells. If you sing and praise his ego then maybe he'll help piss on you after he sets you on fire."

Where was this going? He removed his wire frame glasses. His speech became more animated. More aggressive. I put my hand back in my pocket and on my pistol. The more he spoke, the more I sensed he didn't plan on answering my questions. He continued.

"Then you have this other God." He scoffed. "He is fair and true. There ain't no singing. No dancing. No bullshit rituals. His laws are concrete. They're written in the universe, not on no stone tablet."

"And which do you follow?" I asked him.

"Aren't you listening? I follow the true God. His laws are absolute."

"What's his law?"

"Newton explained it for us. Every action, has a reaction. That's nature."

"Look Steve, let's step inside huh?"

Rain sped down my leather jacket. I began to walk backwards to the house. He yelled out to me as I did so.

"I said I don't want to Detective. We can talk right here or you can leave. Do you have a warrant?"

"No, I'm just here to talk."

"Then you can't enter my property. That's the law, right?"

"You're right."

"Then you can stand right there if you want to talk to me. I work at a school. I'm at the church four times a week. I got nothing to hide."

"Well tell me more about these Gods then."

"The true God never said milk and honey would flow everywhere. Never promised we would live forever. But it did promise that things happen how they happen."

I needed a change of pace. I decided to press.

"I had my own problems with Reverend Brown. Sometimes I wonder which God he follows. What do you think?"

He laughed.

"Reverend Wallace means well. But people like him think that prayer can make everything go away. Singing a song fixes everything. I tried explaining to him..."

His words trailed off.

"Explaining what?"

"You can't pray shit away," he screamed.

I nearly squeezed the trigger. He was certified bat shit crazy. Like mother like son I suppose. He spoke again.

"I know why you're here."

"I told you. I'm looking for Junior."

"He's a good little cat. He's not like his Pop."

I was growing impatient.

"You ever watched a self-righteous person fall? I mean truly fall?"

"I've seen the Reverend," I said.

He smiled and spoke.

"He sits high and mighty. Now, mind you, this is the same man that told me to 'get over it'. Now something happened to him and he's seeing it ain't that easy."

"Get over what Steven?"

This wasn't going to end well I thought. I began to scan the landscape and him. He continued to unravel.

"My so called fucking 'father' tried to kill me before I was born. Didn't even want to meet me and say 'Hey, he's not so bad after all.' He would've rather left me on a bed sheet. And mother? They took her away and let her rot in some looney bin like an animal. How do you–"

At that point he wasn't speaking to me. He was speaking to himself. I think he realized it and stopped talking. He turned his back to me. The rain hitting the water in front of him was strangely calming. I got the feeling he had no intention of letting me inside that trailer.

"I wish for you to leave," he said.

"I'm not going anywhere."

Had he spoken to me like a normal human, I would've left. Cyclops was still my only real suspect, but Steven's behavior put him right up there with him.

"Then it's settled," he said. "It happened so perfect. He was at his breaking point. He learned his lesson. But I got cocky. So now the true God is punishing me. That's the way it goes right? No one can escape–"

"Steven, who is in that trailer?"

"This won't end well Detective. I'm not gonna rot like my mother."

"Steven, this doesn't have to end bad. Where are they?"

"They?" he said.

I aimed the revolver at his back and told him that he was under arrest for kidnapping the two children.

"Get on the ground now. Back away from the water and put

your hands up high where I can see them. Now," I screamed.

"A few more days and it would've been okay. I can't go out like this Detective."

"God damn it. Hands up now," I barked.

I begged him to get on the ground. Not to save his life, but in case he had the kids elsewhere. I needed him alive. He turned towards vegetation to his left. As I figured, he took off running into it.

I yelled at him and gave immediate chase. Branches slapped and clawed at my face and body. Fallen trees stood as obstacles for me to vault over. The marsh like conditions sucked in our feet as we ran. We continued deep into the little forest. I got within ear shot of him and yelled that I would shoot. He stopped dead in his tracks.

From probably twenty, thirty feet away, his back was turned to me. His hands were out to his side. We both panted lightly in the forest.

I went to speak. With the first word out of my mouth, he turned his body. His left shoulder rotated and I saw what looked to be a gun. I let off three shots. The booms echoed throughout the trees. Smoke rolled away from my gun. All I heard was the rain falling on the creek about fifty feet from us.

The force had knocked him on his back. His arm reached out in desperation. With three shots left I scanned the ground for the gun. I kicked at some sticks and leaves and found nothing. I cursed. I knelt down and grabbed him by his flannel collar.

"Where the fuck are they?" I growled at him. He gave a half laugh, half cry.

"I never hurt him. I never would. I was going to let him go I swear."

"Where the fuck are they?"

"He's in the trailer. Tell him I'm sorry."

His words were heavy. He labored to get them out.

"Where is the girl?" I yelled.

I put the pistol under his neck. He looked confused when I mentioned Tasha. Blood oozed out of his side and chest. He had been hit once on his side and twice near his heart it looked like.

He went into shock after that and didn't last another thirty seconds. I added him to the list of souls I had watched depart. I dropped his body and ran to the trailer.

The door was surprisingly strong for a trailer. The door knob slipped through my wet palms as I yanked and pushed on it. I tried my best not to disturb the neighbors but eventually I gave it a strong kick. It burst open and I stepped inside.

Inside, the trailer was immaculate. Almost as well put together as the Reverend's home. It was meager. The walls were a dingy blue, but everything else was lovely. As far as trailers go. Everything was lined up according to size and color. Dishes in the kitchen were put up neatly.

I clicked the TV off. I heard the noise again. I aimed my weapon and followed it to the hall. It might as well have been three football fields long as I inched through it.

The bathroom door was cracked open. I pushed it and pointed the revolver around. Nothing.

To the back of the hallway, I came to the room where I had heard the noise. Of course, the door was locked. I kicked this door open as well and took a step back. Whatever was in the dark room stared down the barrel of my revolver.

"Tasha?" I whispered.

It took my eyes a few seconds to adjust to the dark. The shape of a young child began to appear. I stepped in and turned on the light.

There he was. Wallace Brown Junior was on the floor of the room. Bound at the hands and feet. Tears began to rush out of his innocent eyes. I can't explain it, but I began to cry as well.

I was reminded of a little Vietnamese girl. She sobbed over her father's corpse as we drove away from her village. I felt much of the same then as I did staring at Junior. It didn't matter how tough you were. You'd be a devilish son of a bitch to not feel anything for children. I ripped the tape off his hairless face.

"Are you alright son?" I held him by his face. He was in no position to speak just yet. I grabbed my pocket knife and cut his hands and feet free. He grabbed onto me tight and refused to let go. His nails dug into my skin. I reassured him that he was safe.

I stood up and carried him out the room. I kicked in the door that faced the bathroom. Again, I stepped inside and called out her name.

Nothing inside moved except some angel fish in a tank. Steven's mattress sat on a box spring on the floor. On his wall was a poster of the Greek figure Apollo, holding the world on his back. With my feet and free hand, I flipped his mattress. All the Faygo cans on his night stand hit the wall. I ripped all the clothes out of his small closet and still found no sign of Tasha. Then I remembered the camper out back.

I ran Junior down the steps and out to my car. I laid him down in the backseat and stared at him.

"The girl. Where is she?"

"I didn't see no girl," he said. I wanted to cry just as much as him.

Steven must have kept them separate. I told him to stay there and I would be back.

He screamed for me not to leave him. I slammed the door shut and ran full speed to the blue camper. My soul shook as I stepped inside. To my right was a small kitchen. To the left was a bed.

I hunched over as I entered. The smell alone let me know this was his hunting and fishing storage. Everything you can name was in that trailer. Rifles, ammo, knives, hand guns, bait and poles. Everything except Tasha.

I grabbed one of his revolvers and ran back outside to him. His hands were limp and cold. I placed the revolver in his hand and let him drop it. I needed to clean up the incident. A Negro officer killing a white man wouldn't look too good. Especially not one coming from Detroit.

I can't explain this next part. I've gone over it a million times. I jumped on him and grabbed him by the collar. I put the revolver to his head and screamed at him. His head bobbled back and forth as I shook him.

From behind me, someone yelled at me.

"Drop the weapon and put your fucking hands up where I can see them," it said.

Those where the last words that many Negroes heard. They were usually riddled with bullets right after. I dropped the revolver on Steven's face. My hands went up and hit one of many low lying branches as I turned.

"No, no. Get on the ground with your hands and feet spread out."

I gave them my name and rank. His partner arrived. Two pistols were staring at me.

"Yeah," he said. "And I'm Don Knotts. Now get your black ass on the fucking ground." He crept towards me.

"God damn it. I'm with the Detroit Police. My badge is inside my fucking jacket. This man kidnapped a kid that's in the back seat of-"

"Ahh shut up," his partner told me.

When they got to me, they handcuffed me. They rolled me over on my back. I closed my eyes at the rain drops hitting my face. They pulled my badge out the inside of my jacket.

"Dominique Broddie huh? Well why didn't you say so? What the fuck are you doing out here? Stand up son. What the hell happened?"

I gave them the short version of the story. I was still looking for Tasha. They looked down at Steven and then at me again. I demanded they uncuff me. My thoughts went to Junior.

Had he eaten? Did he need medical attention? Tasha was still out there somewhere. I wanted to tear every square foot of that property up. But right then, I had one kid and I needed to make sure he stayed alive. I turned to Bert and Ernie.

"Have your men search every square fucking foot of this place from top to bottom. Turn those trailers inside out. I don't give a fuck if it's a sacred burial ground. Go no less than five feet down, you dig that?"

They saluted me. I doubt they were military. But even God would've listened to my orders that day. I ran to the car and started it. I reached in the back and rubbed Junior's shoulders.

"You're gonna be okay bud. We'll call your parents and they'll come to the hospital to see you."

It broke me to walk away from that property. But I had to. The boy didn't look too good. Besides, if he was alive, that means Tasha was too.

23

Chapter 23

I think I speak for all Negroes when I say hospitals never felt safe. We had just found out about what they were doing to Negroes down in Tuskegee. They had syphilis but didn't tell the Negroes they had it. Nor did they treat them even when a cure back in the fifties. They kept them in the dark to study its effects.

Every doctor just looked like a damn devil to me. Junior's was hiding his horns as best as he could. His name was Dr. Jacobs. I'm sure he shortened it from Jacobovitz or some shit like that. Though he looked evil, he was surprisingly mild mannered to Junior. I'm sure the presence of a black man who happened to be a cop had something to do with it.

I had been in the room with Junior for about forty-five minutes. I had just gotten off the phone with Carla when the Reverend and his wife crashed through the door.

Talk about a man resurrected. Brown looked to have been given a new body. The white of his eyes was restored. As was his faith in the Lord. The family jumped on Junior and screamed out to the sky in thanks.

Junior grabbed his sisters and pulled them both in tight. The room became warm and full of love. Even the devil smiled at the family.

Reverend Brown peeled away from the reunion and made his way towards me. He looked up at me with tears in his eyes. He uncontrollably wept and pinned his arms around my body. His body jerked up and down as his muffled cries filled the room.

I struggled to get free. He might have actually had the strength of God on his side that day. Eventually I gave in and let him have his moment. The rest of his family joined in.

Finally, he let go of the vice grip. I was able to breathe again. He took a step back and directed me to a corner of the room.

"Detective, wha...what happened?"

"Reverend this might upset you but he was at Steven's house."

He kept repeating the word no and shaking his head. It has to hurt a man's pride to know that someone he trusted would do him so wrong. I stopped him.

"Look in my eyes. I wouldn't lie about something like that."

"Where is he? I'll go see him now."

"It'll be hard to find him. My guess is he probably just now got to the coroner's office."

"No?"

"Yeah. Reverend the man had a vendetta against you."

I explained Steven's philosophy as best I could. I may have gotten the two Gods he explained mixed up but I captured the point. The Reverend didn't seem so shocked about that part.

"I mean, but he was right here through it all. He even helped us look for Junior. I cried on his shoulder for Christ's sake."

"And I'm sure he loved every minute of it. He never spoke to you about his feelings towards God?"

"Well yes but never in that fashion. I thought he was making very fine progress. We got him a plot of land. Helped him find a job. I just, I can't believe this."

"Well his progress was bullshit because I found Junior tied up in a room."

Those words hit the panic button for the Reverend. He shook.

"Oh my God. My boy...You don't think he...?"

His eyes begged for a certain answer.

"No, no. I truly don't. I think he was going to hold onto him until you finally broke. Your boy is fine."

His wife came over to us and cut in.

"I knew that man was no good from the first time I saw him. He just never sat right with me Wallace and I told you that. Why he wanna hang out with Negroes so much anyway? If I could just get my hands on him-"

"Well it doesn't matter anymore. He's gone ma'am. Ain't no use crying over it. He ain't coming back."

"And you're sure he's dead?"

"Yeah. I know a dead man when I see one. I wanted to wait until you got here to ask Junior some questions. Are you both fine with that?"

"Yes of course."

I walked back over towards Junior and hovered over the bed. Soft and gently, I asked Junior what happened. He didn't say anything until I assured him that Steven wouldn't be coming back.

His mother pleaded with him to help. I think she and I were friends by then.

Everything had gone pretty much how the Reverend described to me. Junior went to the store, came back home and went back out. Then he began to fill in the blanks.

"I went to the park before I went back to the store. When I left, Steve pulled up beside me and rolled down the window. He offered me a ride to the store so I got in. But he passed the store and said he was taking me to a big supermarket where everything was fresh."

He stared down at his feet as he spoke. Poor boy.

"He said he asked daddy about it and that it was okay. He said he had to grab money from home so we went to his house. Then he put a blindfold on me and tied my hands and feet."

"Did he do anything to you son?"

"No. He kept giving me food and water. He said he would let me go soon. Are you sure he's not coming back?"

"Yes. I promise you that."

The boy began to tear up. He asked once more for reassurance. Again, I told him.

"He said that he would burn the church and our house down if I said anything. He told me to just be quiet and everything would be okay."

"Steven was a bad man. But my job is to handle bad men like him." I decided to change the pace a bit. "What about the little girl with him?"

"He didn't have no little girl with him. I was in the room the whole time but I never saw or heard no little girl."

"And you're sure about that?"

"Yes sir. I didn't hear or see nobody else."

I stuck my hand out to Junior. He grabbed it and we shook.

"Your family was worried sick about you. They really love you. You're lucky to have such a loving family. I'll come back to check on you later."

I shook the Reverend's hand. Again, he embraced me.

"Where are you going Detective? Where do you think she is?"

"I'm going back to the scene. Hopefully they found something. You can't take a little girl as smart as my Tasha and hide her with no trace. I think she's alive. There'd be no reason to kill one and let the other live right?"

"You're right Detective. The Good Lord will see you through this. I proclaim that she will be found alive."

All Negro Reverends spoke like this. Grand and dramatic. Already, he was back to himself. He continued.

"If there is anything we can do, please let me know. You'll find her. The Lord tells me so."

His daughters came over to me. I knelt down and hugged the adorable duo. I held onto them as if they were Tasha. I felt guilty for hugging someone else's daughter while mine was still missing. I nearly broke down and abruptly took off.

To be honest, their family's happiness pissed me off. My world was still void. I cursed God. I'm sure he was used to it by then. My mother would kill me but that's what I did. He was just fucking with me at that point.

It sounds bad. To find anger in such a joyous family moment. Any other time I would've smiled at the reunion but I had reunited one family while another was still left broken.

24

Chapter 24

Two agonizing days went by. We tossed and turned. Followed up on dead end leads. We had eyes on Cyclops twenty four hours a day. Spoke to half the city and still there had been no sign of Tasha. They turned that entire plot of land upside down and couldn't even come up with a sock. They even sent divers into that choppy creek and followed it for ten miles in each direction. Each time they emerged with tires, shopping carts and busted TVs.

I was stronger than the Reverend. His downward spiral proved that. But maybe his belief system was what kept him from falling completely. God was no longer with me the moment we torched that village. I wondered how much longer I could hold out before I lost it as well.

A dark cloud hovered over me. At times I didn't want to leave the bed. I even had another night terror. It brought me back to the screaming children we often encountered. Some of them would never see their parents again. The stress was getting to me.

And poor Carla. If I was a mess, she was in shambles. I didn't see her eat a solid piece of food for three days. She'd just lay there in bed, not sure of what to do.

Every day the mail lady would drop something off. Carla would hear her and get up and run down the stairs thinking Tasha found her way home. I did my best to get her to stop. But she's a mother. Ain't nothing I could've said in that situation.

On that morning she was still in bed. I was putting on my jeans when she spoke. Her voice bounced off the window she was facing.

"Dom," she said. Her voice was hoarse and choppy.

"Yes?"

"I wish you found her instead. I don't know if that makes me a bad person."

A baseball was lodged in my throat. It began to burn. I didn't know what to say. She spoke again.

"He's older than her. He could've survived on his own. Why Tasha? What was his problem with us?"

"I don't know. Maybe he heard I was asking around."

"You shouldn't have killed him."

I stammered. What could I say to that? He turned like he had a gun.

"Carla, I had to. It was either I shoot him or he would kill me. Then we wouldn't have found either of them."

"Still, you didn't have to."

"We'll find her," I said.

"Why would he hide her somewhere else? Who else could have done this?"

I thought back to Cyclops. His alibis checked out. The only other suspect was Johnnie and he was well on his way to becoming the mayor. He got word about what happened with Steven. My threat to toss him in the river became more serious.

"And that's it?"

"I'm doing all I can. I even went to see Steven's mom."

She sat up.

"What?"

"His mom is in the looney bin in Westland. But it wasn't shit but a waste of time. She just sat there looking crazy. She kept saying his name over and over again."

"Losing a child will do that," Carla said.

"Fuck him. She lost him years ago. They both were just fucking crazy. Even one of his sisters wasn't no help. She was so young when they were separated, she barely remembers him."

"But she has to be somewhere Dom. Someone how to know something. Where is she?"

"I, I don't know. But we'll find her. I found him and we'll find her too."

"But if he's dead, then that means wherever she is, she don't have no food or water. Maybe not even heat."

My throat tightened again. I reached for a glass of water. My voice cracked when I spoke again.

I reminded Carla of the good times we had with Tasha. How Tasha needed us to be strong and to keep looking for her. An idea hatched in my head.

I walked over to the record player and set the spindle on the vinyl. A violin section began to play. After a few seconds Stevie Wonder began to sing about how lovely his daughter had been when she was born.

I pulled Carla by the hand and dragged her to her feet. Her body was heavy and limp. I held her up in my arms and kept her close to me.

"I'm...We're going to find her," I said.

"Promise?"

"I swear to God. I'll light this whole city on fire if I have to."

I'm not sure how long we stood there. But another song was playing when the phone rang downstairs. I nearly tripped over Muddy and everything else in my way as I ran to it. That might have been the longest run of my life.

"Hello?" I said after I snatched it off the hook.

"Dom, its Wendell."

He sounded excited. This was strange for him.

"Dell, what's up?"

"I was calling to check up on you."

My spirit fell into the basement. I immediately lost interest in talking to him.

"We're hanging in there."

He asked how Carla was and other minuscule questions. Then he told me a story.

"I was one of the few Negroes on the police force back then," he said. "I was a bad cop then Dom. I hate to tell it. Did a lot of shit I to this day I'm not proud of. I sabotaged a lot of brothers and hurt them physically and mentally."

So it was true. But I didn't care. He could've killed ten brothers. That was the last thing on my mind.

"I hate to ramble but I say that to say this. It is good to see a good cop who fights against the bullshit we go through. I know you catch flak but you fight the good fight."

I could hear Mitchells in the background.

"I know you are going through a lot but we will find her. She's lucky to have a father like you."

I was speechless. A man expressing something like that was foreign to me. Even if you felt that, you never said it. I wasn't ready to receive those words so they fell flat at the time. All I could muster up was a generic "Thank you."

Looking back, those words kept me going through that day. And boy would I need them.

Hours later I sat at my desk. The longer someone is missing, the harder it was to find them. We all knew that. Wendell had been chasing the case while I focused on Cyclops and Steven. He had dropped off a stack of files of every known child predator within a fifty mile radius. There sure wasn't a lack of suspects.

I began to suspect the guy they were looking for in Oakland County. He was still at large and at the time had been suspected for the deaths of two kids.

I picked through the files of some guy named Tracy Scott. He did a few years for kidnapping and endangering a child. He was from the west side of the city. I was going to go pay him a visit.

Mitchells' phone hit the received loud enough to hear through the closed door. His heavy footsteps were next. They plodded to the door. He swung it open as hard as he could. I froze when he screamed my name.

Believe it or not, he was crying. I looked over at Symanski who looked just as heartbroken as I did. No, no, no. It couldn't be.

I blacked out for a few seconds. When I came to, Mitchells was shaking me. His huge paws slapped my cheek. His mouth was moving but I heard nothing. It was all one long nightmare. Finally, the sound came back.

"Dom, Dom, oh God, wake up. They found her Dom. Get the fuck up," he screamed.

"What? Who?" I was still in a daze.

"Tasha. She's alive son! Somebody found her wandering the streets out in the country. They're taking her to the hospital..."

He said more but I didn't hear any of it. There wasn't a dry eye in that room. I dialed Carla at home.

I called my parents and her's and within two minutes I was down in my car. Where was she? How? I hope she had a jacket on.

I was always a real big tough guy. One of the baddest cats around. I hadn't had a full-fledged cry since I was maybe five years old.

Pop had yelled at me for ruining one of his Billie Holiday records. Then he yelled at me for crying about him yelling at me.

That was my last real cry. One of those cries where your breathing is skipping. It makes you sound like an old sputtering engine. Well it was long overdue.

I cried that day as I flew up Twelfth Street on my way home. I sobbed like a new-born baby. My daughter was alive. That's something to cry over. I don't feel nearly as weak as I thought I would've.

The tires screeched as I made a left onto our street with a trail of fallen leaves behind me. Carla stood at the curb and nearly hopped over the hood to get to the passenger side. It was like we had practiced that many times before. She kissed me and I gave her the rundown as we crossed Eight Mile.

I don't remember anything about the rest of the trip from the time we crossed Eight Mile until we walked into Tasha's room. We ran through the halls to room 317 and pushed aside every doctor and nurse who was in our way.

How would she look? Would she have any scratches? I prayed that she had her jacket with her. When I hit the door, her innocent eyes locked with mine. I made a silent promise that I would never lose sight of them again.

All them tubes and monitors attached to her little body made Carla burst into tears. She went straight to the bed and fell on top of Tasha. The doctor turned around to us.

"You must be Tasha's parents? I'm Doctor Brent Davison."

Carla paid him no mind. She was back on mommy duty. I shook the doctor's hand.

"How, how is she?"

"Well, she was a little dehydrated and hadn't eaten much. She had some mild hypothermia from the cold exposure but she will be just fine."

"Was there any..."

I didn't know how to fully form the question.

"From what we can tell, no Mr. Broddie. There are no signs of any of that."

I walked over to my girls and hugged them both. It almost didn't seem real. Was God playing another trick on me?

Tasha hugged us both and began to cry. It was a tender moment. We had just been reunited with our only child. I had gone to hell and back and even killed a man and nearly killed another looking for her. With all the drama surrounding us, she had the nerve to ask me where Muddy was. I kissed her head and couldn't help but smile. The doctor called out to Carla and I.

"I think we should let Tasha get some rest before any questioning. She was extremely dizzy when she came in. But I would like for you to meet this lovely young woman who found her."

Jesus Christ. How did I not notice a woman sitting in the room the whole time? Good God if she didn't remind me of my grandmother. Her smile. Her full grey Afro. Even down to the moles on her face. We walked over to her. I stood her up and hugged her.

We introduced ourselves. The angel's name was Sherill Clifton.

"How did...Where was she?" I asked.

"I work at the middle school right up the road from where I found her. I was heading home when I saw this poor child walking with just a little jacket on. I had to get out and throw her in my back seat. We went straight to the police station."

"Where was this?"

She gave us the street names and landmarks. I didn't know the area, but I knew it was near Steven's home. I went back to Tasha and touched her cheek and asked her what happened.

Her delicate eyes met mine. Her mouth opened, then closed. Her eyes dropped down to the bed. I grabbed her head and kissed it.

"It's okay baby. Whenever you're ready."

25

Chapter 25

Weeks went by and life began to return to some kind of normal. We pulled Tasha out of that school so fast it wasn't even funny. I'm pretty sure a few other parents followed us.

We decided that we would send her back to school after the Christmas break. Carla took some time off of work and stayed home with her. Whenever I wasn't at work, she'd be lucky to be out of my sight for more than four minutes at a time.

It got so bad to the point where she would just sleep in our room. Man, those first couple of nights were terrible. Our poor little baby really didn't get any sleep, and when she did, them night terrors would wake her right up.

My main man Sam Cooke had a song for every occasion. Many nights I would sing his hit telling us to keep moving on. She liked it but would always request some Stevie Wonder instead. We'd turn the record player on low and let that album play all night. Thankfully those songs calmed her and within minutes, she'd be sleep.

We perched over her like two hawks. What a thing for a child to go through. I would carry my hatred for Steven for the rest of my life. She still would never mention anything about what happened. We figured she'd talk about it when she was ready.

One night in December I decided to get the girls out of the house and go to the precinct's Christmas party. Carla was at her happiest during the holiday season. Christmas music blared through the house as Tasha and I fidgeted in our formal wear while Carla got ready.

All eyes turned to us when I walked in carrying Tasha. I'm not sure if it was because of what we went through, or the fact that Carla had us all wear some sort of matching red. Tasha turned her head from the stares. Just like me, she hated when attention was on her.

Even Symanski showed some humanity in between drinks. He must have voided his Klan card for the night at least.

Wendell's wife was one of the most graceful women I had ever seen. Her processed grey hair hung down to her neck. I always joked with Wendell about how he must've won here in a dice game. She and Carla spoke as women did, while Wendell and I spoke on more important things.

"And when did y'all come up here?" I asked him.

"I was a young gun. I had to be like twelve or something like that."

"Why'd y'all leave?" I caught myself. "I mean, I know why you left but what specifically for your family?"

He scoffed and took a sip of his whiskey. The noise and face he made meant it must have burned going down.

"That's a long, sad story really."

"What else you got to do tonight?"

"Alright. You know the climate in North Carolina back in the early thirties. We were seeing what would eventually become the civil rights movement. It wasn't as organized, but the

205

people were already beginning that defiance."

He coughed and struggled to find his voice. He looked embarrassed at his nervousness.

"My daddy was born in 1901 in a little shack. His grandparents were slaves. Couldn't read and write and all that. So, he took that to heart. By the time daddy was 30, he owned a small newspaper called the Negro Daily Chronicle. It ended up getting him into trouble."

This still evoked memories in him. He paused for a moment, then continued.

"He'd put out the truth and publish the names of men who did lynchings. An 'uppity nigger' that reads and writes was never too high on them white folks' list. There was a Negro in town named Jesse Franklin. Jesse had the smoothest, blackest skin you'd ever want to see. Look at Chelle's dress."

He directed my attention towards Chelle. Her black velvet dress was the talk of the town. She sat there and smiled with some hip looking cat.

"His skin looked just like that. One of them white women liked it a little bit too much, if you catch my drift. The guy she was going with found out. A day later, we found old Jesse swinging from a lamp post in the middle of town. They cut off his-"

He took another sip. I looked over at Tasha. She played with some of the other children. I refused to let her out of my sight anymore. I couldn't look at Wendell. He had tears in his eyes that were close to falling. He kept talking.

"Any way, long story short, daddy published the men's names in his paper. One of them happened to be the sheriff. You know what happens next. One night we are getting ready for bed. We heard some rumbling outside."

He sat up straight and cuffed his hands around his mouth.

"'Percy Wright! Percy Wright! You bring your God damned black ass out here', they said. They said either come with them or they burn the house down. Daddy grabbed his shotgun and went outside alone. Wasn't none of us boys old enough yet to really do anything. Mama held us back as daddy walked out the door. He looked back at us and told us that he'd be back soon. Everything would be okay. We uh, we never saw him alive again. They found him three miles downriver."

Wendell stared at the table.

"Fuck," I said.

"Well, that's why we moved up here in a nutshell. To escape monsters like that."

He had been terrified of whites his whole life. Now I see why he moved up here and became their little pet. Imagine watching that as a child. Seeing them drag your pop off to never be seen again. I couldn't fathom watching my Pop taken away. I would've come out blasting. I decided to change the topic from murder.

"My pop had a friend back in the day. One of the few handpicked Negroes they allowed to live in Gross Pointe. We'd go to visit him every now and then. They'd debate on whatever they talked about at the time."

"He must have been a doctor or something?"

"Yeah he was. We were coming back from his place one night and Pop made a wrong turn. So he's driving slow to find his way back. No harm, right? We're going maybe twenty-five in a thirty-five when we get pulled over."

I turned my attention from Tasha.

"We already knew what it was about. You know that fat son of a bitch ticketed Pop for driving too slow. Can you believe that? Too slow?"

"That ain't surprising. What time of day was it?"

"Like eight at night."

He laughed and spoke.

"Especially that late. You know Negroes couldn't be caught there after sundown at one point. The north was full of them kind of places. Probably still is."

"It ain't no better up here than it is in the south," I said matter of factly.

He raised his eyes from the table.

"Oh no. It's much better. They're just as racist up here. But I ain't seen no Negro swinging from a tree yet."

I felt a tap on my leg when I went to respond. I picked Tasha up and sat her on my knee. I gave Wendell the look that mean we would finish that later. It was for the best. His mind was in another place by now.

"What's wrong, baby?" I asked Tasha.

She laid her head on my shoulder. I spoke her language. She was ready to leave. Symanski staggered over to our table.

He had solved the Lyles case a few weeks prior. My old friend Johnnie Parlor called and gave me a tip that I passed on. They found them four boys in some rundown apartment building in Highland Park. You'd think they'd run to a different state at least. I guess Highland Park is technically another city, even though Detroit completely surrounds it.

The strangest part is known of them had any known gang ties. It turns out they just did it, just to do it. Only three of them were in jail and waited for trial. The fourth took off and was used as target practice. Symanski was probably on his way to a promotion but I didn't really care too much about being on the case. I had my little girl back, and I could rise through the ranks some other way. Until then, the best way for me to help the city was to do my parts as a detective and father.

Symanski greeted us all at the table.

"This party is really happenin' huh? Hi little lady. I'm so glad you're safe. I work with your daddy."

I told her to say hi to him. She was never shy before. Perhaps she had been too trusting. She gave a guarded wave and turned back to me. She wasn't in the mood to meet new adults just yet. Symanski's wife stepped in.

"You'll have to excuse George. He threw back one too many so we're going to head home a little early. You all get home safe. Come on George."

Her frustration with him was apparent. He muttered to himself and stutter stepped as she dragged him by the ear from table to table. Wendell looked up at me.

"You know, even Symanski was going around trying to gather info on her. I guess he ain't all bad."

"Yeah, neither was Nixon. You see where that got us. I'm gone wean you off them white folks one day," I smiled at him.

We left the party around nine. Downtown was beaming with lights that crawled up the high-rise buildings and trees. Tasha could use some Christmas joy. Hell we all could. We parked and walked up and down Woodward in this winter paradise.

Tasha smiled at the Christmas wreaths that wrapped hung on the lamp posts. The holiday season gave a brief escape from the racial tensions that gripped the city. For these few weeks, everyone was less on edge. A white family had been enjoying the night just as we were. We both waved and smiled at each other. I wondered if that would have been the case six months earlier.

The Hudson's department store was the epicenter of the

crowd. Lights in the shape of a Christmas tree climbed up nine out of the twelve stories and invited shoppers inside. That night, Tasha wasn't having it but a winter wonderland was inside. It was a child's dream. As jumping as the scene was, it was nothing compared to when I was a child.

The whites had begun to leave the city in droves for about thirty years at that point. I thought about what that could mean for the city's future. It was sized for two million people. A loss of that many-. I caught myself. This was a family night.

Tasha was even more worn out when we got to the car. Her eyes sparkled from the city lights outside the window. Call it strange, but I didn't like for her to think too much those days. I didn't want her to think about what happened. Maybe she didn't feel safe anymore.

Children don't process like we do. Steven was a piece of human garbage. But she didn't know that. She would blame me or even worse, blame herself.

"What's on your mind baby girl?" I interrupted.

"Nothing."

"No. You can tell us anything. What's up?"

"It's your partner. The old guy."

"What about him?"

"He smelled like that man."

Symanski had been drinking whiskey that night. My body went numb. I didn't need her to explain which man. I'd bring him back and kill him again if I could.

But then it hit me. Steven didn't drink. They didn't find anything other than water and juice in his trailer. The smell of cheap whiskey. Who smelled like that?

My mouth remained pinned shut the entire ride home. I tried to open it but each time I stopped myself. I knew what would come out. Carla had to be able to hear my heart pounding.

I began to shake, but I kept my cool. All the houses on our block were lit up. Carla pointed out the various decorations as we pulled into our driveway. We went inside and I put the girls to sleep in our room. I grabbed my keys and tip toed out the front door. I was going to close this case.

26

Chapter 26

It was near midnight when I pulled up. The light to the office in the back of the building was still on. What's the old saying? There's no rest for the wicked? Looking at it from that way, it made sense that Brown was still awake.

He probably was inside planning his next move. Preparing to take another child or continue to cover up what he had done. They all warned me about this two-bit son of a bitch. I knew he was a lying bastard. But I allowed him to slip in right from under me. A man who can't protect his children isn't fit to be a father and honestly that made me feel lower than when she was gone.

But why? Why had he taken her? Was it because his child was gone so he wanted me to share in on the misery? Or was it because he thought I wasn't taking it serious? I could've sat there for four more hours pondering the whys and hows but I decided to go and confront the problem.

I got out my car and felt for the revolver. It was always there when I needed it. The temperature chilled to the bone that night. I didn't feel a thing. I was so hot that all I wore was a small jacket.

I knocked at the side door and waited for a while. No answer. Punk motherfucker probably thought a demon was at the door. I guess he'd be half right.

The longer I waited, the angrier I got. I balled my fist and pounded against the metal screen. The lock clicked and the door cracked open. Those beady eyes stared at me through the slit.

"Detective, what on God's green earth brings you here this late?"

"Let me in, Wallace."

"Uh what's this about? We're upstairs sleeping."

"You ain't sleep."

He pulled the door open and unlocked the screen door. I walked in and scanned around. I don't know what I had been looking for. But when I found it, I just knew I would know.

He led me back to his office and sat down in his chair.

"I'm glad to see you again. Is uh, everything alright?"

His hands sat on his newly gained belly. They fidgeted as he picked his nails. I noticed the decaying smell of flesh and whiskey was gone. I breathed deeply for the first time around him.

"I didn't want much. I came to see how you and the family were."

"At midnight?"

"Yeah. I was out with my family and thought about Junior. I couldn't wait."

He echoed the midnight sentiment.

"I figured you'd be up. And here you are," I said. "Men like us don't get to sleep much."

"Yes well, how, how's Tasha doing?"

"Good. Don't let her out of my sight anymore. There are weirdos out here. She still hasn't said much."

"Do you have any leads?"

His voice cracked.

"A couple. One major lead. But I'm keeping it classified until I've got something concrete."

"Yeah, yeah, I don't let Junior or the girls out my sight as well. I'm actually glad you're here. I need to ask you something."

Oh, that son of a bitch was good. He was going to divert my attention. "Two-bit, pulpit pimp".

"Go ahead," I said.

"Well, you see, after all my years here, I never felt that I needed a gun until now. It's becoming sadly apparent that even God's word isn't enough to scare off the wolves."

"I agree," I said.

"Now I'm not doubting His awesomeness, but it concerns me. How could someone do this to our children? How long had he been planning this? When it comes to guns-"

I decided to answer the first question.

"When we were in Vietnam we quickly learned a vital lesson. I seemed to have let it slip recently. Your enemy could always be right next to you and you would never know it."

"How's that?"

"The jungle was so thick. In some places, a whole squad could be ten feet away. You'd never know until one of them sneezed or moved. Your enemy is always close to you."

"That's what scares me the most because who is next? I disbanded all my community programs. I can't look at people in my own church the same. We're even considering getting out of here. Maybe heading out West. It's really hindered my peace."

"Yeah. A trusted person taking advantage of you like that can fuck you up. You know Wallace, I been meaning to ask you some things."

He raised his eyebrow. His hands were picking at his fingers at a furious pace.

"During my investigation, I ran across some disturbing news about you."

"What about?"

"That you're a fraud."

"You know? I'm not surprised. Most people love to focus on the bad you do. They skip right over the good. What'd they say? I was engaged in some shady business when I was young? Ok. So what? We all were."

He took off his glasses and tossed them on the desk. Our shadows looked huge in the room.

"You know what sounds good to the press? 'Criminal Turned Priest' sounds better than 'Priest Making a Difference in the Neighborhood'. Them folks are only focused on the negative a man does in his life. If we stuck with that, we never would've had Brother Malcolm."

I let a laugh escape me.

"You ain't no Malcolm," I said.

"You're smart enough to understand context, right? I'll tell you this. I ain't never hurt nobody. Not a soul. Anything I ever did was what needed to be done. When I go in front of St. Peter, they won't tie my soul to any physical or spiritual wounds. Can you say the same?"

Like I said. He was good. But I was better.

"Unfortunately, no. I can't. I killed a man to get Junior back. I have killed more men than 100 of your average guys. I've harmed even more."

"You're a father. Soldier. Detective. I'm sure there are certain things with your job that you wished you never did, right? But you did it because you had to protect something or someone."

"Of course, Wallace."

"So then step outside of yourself and walk in my shoes. My son was-"

"You were out of line Wallace."

He began to sweat.

"You have to understand I-"

I reached inside my coat and whipped the revolver out. Four pounds of steel stared at him. He squirmed and fell backwards. He scurried into the corner like a roach.

"Now you repent," I told him. "You tell me about my sins? I suggest you start right now."

He jumped to his knees and bowed and began to pray to some God. I hated to admit it but I saw what Steven was saying. The God Wallace believed in allowed him to take children. He believed in something completely different.

I won't say killing a man gets easy. One of two things happens. You come up with crazy notions to justify it. Or, you figure your soul is damned anyway so what's one more going to do?

What are they gonna do? Throw you in super hell? Turn the fire up a little hotter? I didn't care about shooting a man of God. He wasn't one. On his knees in that corner, I think he finally realized that. I cocked the hammer.

"She's seven you son of a bitch."

"I had to Dom. You weren't taking me serious before. She didn't eat much of the food we gave her but she was never in any danger. Look, we're the same. We would do anything for our kids."

"I ain't shit like you."

"I had to," he pleaded. "I love my family as much as you. What would you have done?"

Something caught my eye on his bookcase. It was a large orange square. It was that fucking Stevie Wonder album. Men like him and Steven didn't deserve to live among us. We needed men to sacrifice their own souls to take them out.

But if I shot him right then and there, I would never hear Tasha sing those songs again. The .357 rattled in my hands. I'd miss birthdays. Holidays. Even just being there in the morning took on a new importance after our ordeal. What's worse is I wouldn't be there to protect her anymore. She and Carla needed me then more than ever.

We caught a VC sniper who had killed five of our guys in a month. We did some pretty rough things to him. Things I wanted to do to Wallace that night. I hated Wallace even more than I hated him. I could argue God or wherever we went when we died about it. I'd say it to their face that I did no wrong.

I lowered the gun. The relief on his face made my blood boil. I put it back in my pocket and stormed over to him. I blacked out and when I came to, his face wasn't recognizable. Blood stained his white t shirt and he covered himself in a ball of pity. I grabbed him by the collar.

"If I ever hear anything else from or about you, they won't find your body for another two hundred years at the bottom of the fucking river."

I doubted that he'd be able to see out of that eye again. He certainly wouldn't breathe right again. For good measure, I pulled out my pocket knife. He whimpered and winced as I cut a gash across his cheek. Hopefully it would serve as a reminder until he was hit by a car or some dope fiend killed him, or whatever end a man like him deserves.

I tossed him back to the floor and turned to his desk. With one swipe, I knocked everything off it. I reached for the book shelf. Every theology book was tossed at him.

He had a picture of him and the man himself. Sam Cooke smiled while Wallace had his arm around him. I snapped the frame and pulled out my lighter. Sam's face melted away before I threw the photo onto him.

I performed a scorched earth policy on my way out of the building. I went so far as to take a screw driver to his tires. Complete with a brick through his car window.

When I got back to my car I looked over at the church. I could've burned it down right then. No one would've suspected it was me. I could go slit his throat. Make it look like a murder-suicide. A millions schemes ran through my mind on what I could do.

I wanted to toss him in the river. They'd find his body in Toledo in fifty years. But instead, I turned the key in the ignition and drove off. Did I do the right thing? I don't know. It might have been a smart move. Or maybe I was getting soft as I got older.

27

Chapter 27

Six months went by. Tasha's road to recovery was a concentrated effort that took a toll on all of us. Staying in her room all night. Being there ten minutes early to pick her up from school. But by the summer, she began to get back to her normal self.

"Now don't go over there asking your grandma for any money," I said to Tasha while looking in the rear-view mirror. She hung her head low.

"Aw, why not?"

"You just be extorting her cause you know she won't tell you no. Got us looking like we ain't feeding you."

"What's extorting mean?"

"What money they give her ain't none of your business, Dom," said Carla.

"It's all my business when she ain't buying nothing but candy with it and I get a dentist bill. They could at least put it in a college fund."

"You just mad cause they didn't give you nothing when you were a kid," she smiled.

"They gave me a good education of life in the streets. That

was all I needed."

Sunday dinners were a tradition in our family. My parents were close with their siblings. My dad alone had five brothers. Uncles Freddie, Charles, Leon, Frank and Ron. Aunts Raven, Genny, cousin Bobby and more would all show up. We'd packed my parents' west side house with nothing but love.

Pops and I kept their lawn immaculate. He'd always say "A man's house is his pride." I never understood it until I got my own crib. That summer me and my girls zipped down the road without a care in the world.

The scene was beautiful when we pulled up. Kids were in the street tossing the football around. They hit a car and scattered when a pissed off Mrs. Tanner ran outside after them.

Mr. Graham was directly across the street. He walked behind his lawnmower for the fifth time that week. Him and Pop had to be in competition. He wiped his forehead and waved at us.

Next door Mrs. Rose sat on her porch with her daughter. The radio was blasting "Got To Give It Up" by brother Marvin.

Everybody wanted to be down with Motown. You could camp out and watch all them Motown acts go in and out of the Hitsville building. We grew up with some of them so seeing them perform on TV was out of sight.

Tasha and Muddy jumped out the backseat and straight to the front door. Carla screamed and everything in the neighborhood came to a standstill. I swear the football stopped in midair.

Tasha knew what she meant. Her and Muddy dropped their ears and went around back to keep him outside. Old Negro women do not like pets for some reason. My mom was no different.

Mom and pop had a huge house on a long corner lot. Tasha and Muddy ran along the fence to the backyard. An ungodly amount of cousins eagerly awaited her. I got out the car. Mr. Graham shut off his mower and yelled out to me.

"How I'm looking young blood?" he gestured to his yard.

"Better than last time," I smiled.

"Awh you don't know nothing. Ain't a golf course within fifty miles looking better than this here!"

I went around the car and opened Carla's door. She grabbed onto my arm and struggled to pull herself out. I held her hand as she waddled to the front door. She rubbed her bowling ball stomach.

From the moment we found out, I wouldn't even let her walk by herself. It was the same way when she was pregnant with Tasha. No walking during the winter in snow and ice. I waited on her hand and foot.

She knew not to get used to it though. I think she was one of the only few women who enjoyed being pregnant. Mom stood at the front door wiping her hands on a towel.

"Girl how far along are you? Three months?"

She always said something like that to make Carla feel better. Truth be told, she was huge. She didn't speak to me for two weeks when I told her.

That had to be a boy in there. A boxer. With a long left jab. I could see it already. I picked up one of the knocked over pots on the porch and walked inside.

I kissed mom on the cheek and greeted everyone. And I mean everyone. Even Wendell took me up on my invitation. Him and Pop sat in the back watching baseball.

Them old Negroes trashing some white boy pitcher called "The Bird"? That was worth showing up alone. "He ain't no Satchell Paige", is all Pop said the whole damn game. I just waiting for someone to mention Rocky Marciano.

The next three hours were full of nothing but laughing and eating. Uncle Chuck and Aunt Barbara were always the center of attention. When we grew bored with them, cousins Harold and Shawn's drunk arguments picked up the slack. My cousin Pete was never too far away, telling anyone who would listen about his latest get rich quick scheme.

Carla's brother was my favorite character. There wasn't a woman within 100 miles who didn't know who he was. The brother was smooth. Even on a trip to the gas station, he was Mack Daddy fresh. He sat in the den with his legs crossed while his girl of the week tended to his every want.

These dinners were important to us. They kept us close. It felt like the world was becoming so fast-paced. It was tough to make time to sit down with each other. They did it back in the day all the time.

They would sit at the dinner table. Fathers knew every part of their family. They didn't have any bullshit to distract them. I often wondered if I was romanticizing.

Them Sunday dinners were like church services. They put a shield of armor on us. Our souls would need protection for the upcoming week. Especially for the years to come. I was becoming poetic from the books Carla had me reading.

The sun went down. The muggy heat of the day turned into a comfortable night breeze. I looked around for pop. He sat in the backyard watching the kids play basketball.

Next to him was his old blue Ford Econoline van. I plopped next to him.

"When you gonna get rid of that thing?"

"Get rid of it? That's a mighty fine vehicle."

"Pop you ain't been able to start it in over ten years.

"It just needs a good belt."

"Little junior gone be driving that before you get it working."

"Who asked you? Speaking of that, how's he doing?"

"He's good. She's so big, it has to be a boy. I'm hoping it's a boy. She said he kicks strong. I'll make him a boxer for sure."

"Boxer, soldier, business man, he'll be something."

"He ain't gonna be no soldier Pop. Businessman for sure."

"I hear that son. It's just something about soldering that builds a man."

"Speaking of that, I been meaning to ask you this for years."

My palms greased themselves. This was the man closet to me. But I felt like a stranger trying to ask him this. I know, it's my father. If I couldn't talk to him then who could I talk to? But men were different back then.

"Did you ever kill anyone?"

He took a sip of his beer. His response was delayed. I could tell that he had spent a lot of time thinking about this.

"Of course."

"Do you ever regret it?"

"It's not a regret. It's more that I wish I wasn't in the situation to have had to do it."

A group of children ran by the fence and traced it with their fingers. Pop playfully yelled out and they took off running. He turned back to the basketball game and spoke.

"Well, I guess that is regret."

"What?"

"I don't regret that I did it. I regret I was the one to have to do it."

The riddle stumped me.

"Huh?" I asked.

"Look, it haunted me real bad at first. I can remember his face. You remember my buddy George Hummel?"

223

"The guy with no pinky finger?"

"That's him. He was there with me. George was my best friend. It was 1945 when we rode into Gunskircheln concentration camp. Boy were them Jews happy to see us. They ran up to the fence half naked and climbed to get to us. Memories like that take away my regret."

"That's the biggest problem with our war. We ain't have no saving moment like that. We didn't even know who we were saving. I saw all that footage with Walter Cronkite. Y'all had them big tanks rolling through the countryside. All the people screaming and showing you love and praise. I thought it'd be the same when I got to Vietnam."

"What was it like?"

This was the first time we spoke on our experiences. Any other time when I was young, pop would say "some other time son" and send me away.

"I looked for a welcome party. There wasn't no music, no paved streets, no big buildings. I thought for sure these little brown women would show up and give me gifts. Outside of Saigon, there were only little straw huts. All their cattle stood right outside the doors, damn near in the houses. Pop, I went over there thinking they were horrible monsters. Seven feet tall with fangs."

I spread my arms up high to demonstrate the height.

"But pop, they were so fu-so freaking strange to me. They talked like cats. They were short. They only came up to this tall." I held my hand up to my shoulder. "And usually not even that much. And pop, they smelled strange. The whole damn country smelled strange. To try to get it on with a woman there, you'd have to worry about the smell. Well, it's not that they smelled bad, just different."

"It was like that with them Frenchies too. We all use different soap and shit I guess, but them white boys smelled like wet dogs sometimes." He took a pause. "I never told you this but I was disappointed when you went off."

"Really? I went to try to make you proud."

"Well that was just fucking stupid son."

We burst out laughing.

"Do you miss it sometimes?" I asked.

"You know, I thought that as I grew older, I'd become a monk. Somebody who loved peace and never longed for violence. But I do miss it. Sadly. I miss doing the shooting. I even miss getting shot at. I guess that's only due to me living. I'm sure some of them dead boys would tell you different. I miss the feeling in France."

"What feeling?"

"Like God damn movie stars. Them white women loved them some Negroes and wasn't shy to tell it. That was enough to get you hung over here. Them Negroes from the south were banging with a vengeance."

I didn't want to speak on the Vietnamese women. They weren't as willing as the French and I saw many men do terrible things. Of all the horror I've done, that was one thing no one could put on me. Pop continued.

"Them white boys told the French women that Negroes had tails to scare them off. Well it made them curious and we showed them what else we got. It was like a kid in a candy store."

"Y'all were running around like that Pop?"

"You better believe it. Well, they were. I'm a happily married man," he smiled. "It pissed them white boys off. I would've stayed over there if I could've."

225

"But aren't they just as racist? They had slaves and took over Africa too."

"Good point. I guess they were just nicer because they knew we weren't staying."

"Yeah. They knew you were going home eventually. If you stayed in large numbers, you'd see something different."

"Look Negative Nancy, whatever the reason, it made a lot of men say fuck the US. You had a whole bunch of pissed off fighters coming back. That's when the civil rights got started. With the men coming back saying fuck that. But what were we saying?"

"I was saying how my war didn't have no saving moment."

"Oh yeah. Hitler was the devil himself. I could stomach losing you if you went to fight the devil. But I just don't feel the same about Vietnam."

"We even wondered why we were there. Once them thoughts came, I knew it was time to get out. After two years, my heart wasn't in it no more. All the things we did was just..."

I grew animated. I caught myself and sat back. Pop spoke.

"War ain't natural son. Well I guess it is, but the human mind ain't prepared to see all that shit. That's why they desensitize you. Make you less than human."

I shook my head in agreement.

"It's easier to kill a blood thirsty communist, than it is a rice farmer who wants to protect his family. I don't envy you boys at all. We had a face to focus on and hate. Hitler was taking anything he wanted to. I can justify killing a man to save others."

"That's the thing. What did I do it for? To stop Communism? I try fighting them feelings but-"

"Ahh don't fight that shit. Everything ain't a battle. You did what you did and it's over now. Do you feel bad about it?"

"Yeah."

"Then ain't no need in beating yourself up. Some men belong in the world and some don't. Men like us keep everyone safe and do our part. I think God understands that."

"You think so?"

"I sure do hope so. All you can do is repent. And make sure we don't make the same mistake twice and ruin more lives. If you really feel bad, then donate some money or something."

"It's hard to not think about it. Them men had families."

"So do you."

"But we invaded them. They're people just like us. Like, like this one little cat. His name was Chi. He told me that the South Vietnamese wouldn't walk next to us Americans."

I stood up and stood at attention like Chi used to do, when speaking to us. I did my best to mimic his American accent.

"Now I'm thinking how sweet of them. To want to keep us safe. I found out later that they did this because we were so much taller, snipers could see us easier. They didn't want to take a bullet meant for us."

We laughed again.

"But see? You got something out of it. They aren't just people you hear about. You've seen them. Ate with them. That's the joy of traveling. We ain't no different."

"I thought that all the traveling I did, all I've done with life, that I'd feel different you know? More complete. I even joined the force to get that wartime excitement back. I just feel empty."

"Empty?"

Remember, Pop was from a different era. Sympathy and understanding were for sissies. As rough as he was, he always made time to listen.

"Yeah. We'll be at Belle Isle and it's gorgeous outside. Like I should be happy but I feel nothing. Literal nothing. Or we go to a concert and the crowd and loud noises end up pissing me off. Then we have to leave early cause of me and I know Carla is upset but won't say so."

Pop didn't speak. His war was different.

"Or that I have to sleep with a night light. I'm a grown man with a night light. I can't eat sometimes. Even mom's macaroni just tastes bland sometimes. I thought—"

"Look son, I don't think it will ever go away. Men like us? We're protectors. Protectors of the country, ourselves and our families. I hate to tell you but you have to learn to deal with it. Man up."

He took a sip of beer and took off his hat. His shiny head was sweating. He just started to lose his hair. He turned to me.

"You ain't no average man. You can bear the load. You did it so others didn't have to. They couldn't handle it like you. You think I cut my grass because I like it? It gives me something to do. A purpose so I ain't cooped up in that house thinking all damn day. Ain't nothing that pulls you out of it?"

"I guess Tasha and now Carla."

"Then you use that. Those are your reasons. You learn to see who you are still alive for and who needs you. It won't make it go away, but trust me, it helps."

I grabbed a sheet of paper towel from the table in front of us and wiped my face with it.

"I hope I'm doing good with this fatherhood thing. I just feel so horrible it happened to her. Now I feel like I'm over parenting."

"That was a special case. But you found her. Ain't no manual for being a dad because there ain't no one way to raise a kid. You figure shit out as you go along."

I shook my head and he spoke again.

"I didn't know what the fuck to do with you when we brought you home. I almost put you in a drawer to sleep."

"In a drawer pop?"

"Hey, I said there was no manual."

"I really do hope she's having a boy. I hope he'll grow up to protect his sister and mom when I'm gone."

Pop stood up and did something unexpected. He was every bit as big as I was. He stood me up and wrapped his arms around me.

The hug was stiff and awkward for both of us. I wondered what my granddaddy would have said if he seen that. Men were different back then. I could've cried right there.

Then he let me go and we sat back down. He spoke.

"Son, I think that boy will grow up to be just fine."

The End.

About the Author

Born in Detroit, D'Andre Walker went on to graduate from Michigan State University. A civil engineer by day & hard hitting amateur boxer by night, D'Andre decided to write novels to ensure positive and accurate portrayals of the African American experience. Known for his love of boxing, hunting and the outdoors, D'Andre can always be found in a gym or out on a hiking trail trying to avoid snakes.

You can connect with me on:

🔲 https://www.facebook.com/DreWalkTheAuthor

Also by DAndre Walker

Not Only in Blood

A coming of age tale that highlights the struggles of adolescence during pre-Emancipation America, Not Only in Blood offers a fresh new perspective on the era from voices that have rarely been given prominence. In the year 1825, "the boy" lives a life that most fifteen year olds could only dream of. His parents are wealthy, he can read, write and most of all, he was born free. Still feeling shackled by society, he runs away from the sheltered home he grew up in and finds himself on the American frontier. Here he is thrust into a frightening world that allows very few men to live to tell of its beauties...and its horrors.

CPSIA information can be obtained
at www.ICGtesting.com
Printed in the USA
LVHW031736300421
686100LV00004B/105